beneath a meth
moon

AN ELEGY

beneath a meth
moon

AN ELEGY

JACQUELINE WOODSON

NANCY PAULSEN BOOKS   AN IMPRINT OF PENGUIN GROUP (USA) INC.

NANCY PAULSEN BOOKS

A division of Penguin Young Readers Group.

Published by The Penguin Group.

Penguin Group (USA) Inc., 375 Hudson Street, New York, NY 10014, U.S.A.

Penguin Group (Canada), 90 Eglinton Avenue East, Suite 700, Toronto, Ontario M4P 2Y3,
Canada (a division of Pearson Penguin Canada Inc.).

Penguin Books Ltd, 80 Strand, London WC2R 0RL, England.

Penguin Ireland, 25 St. Stephen's Green, Dublin 2, Ireland (a division of Penguin Books Ltd).

Penguin Group (Australia), 250 Camberwell Road, Camberwell, Victoria 3124, Australia
(a division of Pearson Australia Group Pty Ltd).

Penguin Books India Pvt Ltd, 11 Community Centre, Panchsheel Park, New Delhi—110 017, India.

Penguin Group (NZ), 67 Apollo Drive, Rosedale, Auckland 0632, New Zealand
(a division of Pearson New Zealand Ltd).

Penguin Books (South Africa) (Pty) Ltd, 24 Sturdee Avenue, Rosebank,
Johannesburg 2196, South Africa.

Penguin Books Ltd, Registered Offices: 80 Strand, London WC2R 0RL, England.

Published simultaneously in Canada. Printed in the United States of America.
Design by Ryan Thomann. Text set in Chaparral Regular.

Library of Congress Cataloging-in-Publication Data is available upon request.
ISBN 978-0-399-25250-1

2 4 6 8 10 9 7 5 3 1

for my mom and grandma, in memory

and for my sister, Odella

Before I traveled my road, I was my road . . .

—Antonio Porchia

This road . . .

IT'S ALMOST WINTER AGAIN *and the cold moves through this town like water washing over us. My coat is a gift from my father, white and filled with feathers. My hair is healthy again and the wind whips the white-blond strands of it over my face and into my eyes so that from far away, I must look like some pale ghost standing at the corner of Holland and Ankeny, right where the railroad track moves through Galilee, then on to bigger towns. My hands pressing the small black notebook to my chest, my head back, eyes closed against the wind and early falling snow. This is me now. This is me on this new road . . .*

Later, I'll write this down—how early the snow

came, how surprising, how the flakes drifted white and perfect around me. I'll write, "The moon was finally out of me, and maybe because of this, everything felt new and clean and good . . ."

In the distance, I hear a train whistle blowing— coming from far off. But fast-moving . . . toward me.

On days like this, with so much beauty circling me, it's hard not to feel a hundred years old. Hard not to let the past come raining down. Hard not to think about not deserving this kind of beauty, this kind of cold. This . . . this clarity. But Moses and Kaylee keep telling me that fifteen is just another beginning, like the poet with the two roads and his own choice about which one he'd be taking. You got a whole lot of roads, *Kaylee says to me. And some days, I believe her. As I walk down this one . . . I believe her.*

Kaylee says, Write an elegy to the past . . . and move on. *She says it's all about moving on.* I've read about it, Laurel. You write all the time. You can do this.

So I'll begin it this way—It's almost winter again . . .

Soon, Moses will join me here. He'll walk along these tracks with his bag slapping against the side of him. He'll see me in my white coat and smile. He'll see me here—living. Something neither one of us can hardly believe.

Together we'll sit by the edge of the tracks and talk real quiet about moving forward—over that crazy year. I'll put my head on his shoulder and tell him again about my life in Pass Christian, the house we lived in there, my mama, about Jesse Jr. being born fast in the night. About M'lady.

And Moses, my brother-friend . . . Moses, my anchor and my shore, will lift the collar of my coat higher up around my ears, pull my hat from my pocket and make me put it on.

I'm painting over those snowflakes, *Moses will say.* One by one, they're slowly fading out of here.

As I begin this story, I believe him.

moses

THE FIRST TIME MOSES dropped a dollar in my cup, I didn't even know his name. I looked up at him, glad for the dollar. Maybe I said thanks, but it's blurry sometimes, my memory is. One moment clear as water, then another moment, and it's like somebody's erasing bits and pieces of it.

What I'm seeing as I write this down are the shadows, brown and black and some kind of blue that maybe was the jacket he was wearing, a can of spray paint in one hand, a brush in his other. Maybe it was night. Maybe I asked him his name, because he said, *I'm Moses.* And I said, *Then this must be the promised land.* The Bible comes to me that way—quick and sharp like a pain. I had just turned fifteen, and with it came a new way of talking and smiling to get what I wanted. Maybe I was thinking I could get another two dollars out of his pockets.

But Moses just looked at me like he was looking at someone familiar and strange at the same time. Most kids just passed me by, laughing, sometimes throwing whatever they're carrying at me—half a candy bar, an empty potato chip bag, a soda can. But Moses stopped, looked at me, put that dollar in my cup, said, *Did you know Ben? I'm painting that wall for his mom.*

Maybe I knew right then he was different.

No, I said. *I don't know anybody by that name.*

She wants it to say "Ben, 1995–2009. We'll always wonder about the man you could've been," Moses said. *Then she wants me to put "We love you forever" at the bottom. In small letters. Like she's whispering it to him. That's what she said—"Like I'm whispering it."*

You can hardly see it with the sun almost down. Moses pointed at the wall. *Beauty wasted,* he said. *Look at him.*

Maybe I squinted across where the painting was getting started. Maybe I saw a pale outline—the beginning of the ending of Ben. It didn't mean anything to me, though.

I asked Moses if he played ball, because he looked real tall standing there, and I figured he might have seen me cheering. I was hard to miss on the court. At least that's what people said, but I saw the way his smile went away.

We don't all *play ball,* he said.

I would have asked him about this *we all* thing. But other people started passing by, and I needed to make some money. *You stay blessed, Moses,* I said, by way of saying "good-bye, now," but trying not to be rude because he had dollars he was sharing with strangers.

Maybe I smiled, because he looked at me again for a quick second, and I think that was because of where T-Boom chipped my tooth when we were still together. T-Boom's got the whole tooth missing, and after we knocked out each other's teeth, I guess we figured there wasn't anything left to do, so we stopped going out. But of course I still saw him—sometimes two or three times a day.

Moses had his girl with him. She looked down at me like I didn't even have a right to be living, but

I just gave the look right back to her. She took her phone out of her pocket and dialed a number, said *Hey, baby,* then turned away from us, talking real quiet into it.

You must have some people somewhere, Moses said.

I pulled my top lip down over the chipped tooth, looked away from him and shook my head. I hadn't felt any shame about that tooth before and didn't know why I was feeling it now.

My people are gone.

Gone dead, Moses asked, *or gone gone?*

Both.

He nodded, squinting at me like he was trying to put some puzzle together.

The girl put the phone in her bag and turned back around, pulling at his arm, saying they were gonna be late. She talked like she'd been schooled in the real right way to say things: "We're. Going. To. Be. Late. Moses."

I'll be back around to work on that wall tomorrow, he said to me, then let his girl pull him out of my line of vision.

And I guess I forgot about him, because it was

getting real cold and I was thinking about getting to the House before T-Boom went home to his own mama and ate her dinner, then watched some of his mama's TV and went to bed in the room he grew up in. And once the House closed, you couldn't go looking for T-Boom at his mama's because she didn't know anything about where his money was coming from, so I let myself shiver until a few more quarters and dollars fell into my hat and then I put my sign away in my bag, blew my nose on my bandanna and packed up shop for the night. I got up and shook my legs to get the blood running back through them. The fuzz went away from my mind. A lady and man were walking toward me, and for a quick minute I smiled, thinking, *Here comes my daddy. Coming to take me home.* But then the man just patted his pockets and gave me one of those *I'm sorry* looks. The woman didn't look at me at all. I stood there watching them move quick past where I was standing. Something got hard and heavy inside of me, and I knew real deep that my daddy wasn't coming here to get me. Not this time. Not anymore.

the house

THE HOUSE WAS DARK by the time I hitched and walked the four miles to it. Another four miles past it and I'd be at my own house—where maybe my daddy and Jesse Jr. were sitting down in front of the television, eating spaghetti with sauce from a jar. No green vegetables to speak of, like how it would be if I was still living with them. It had been weeks, maybe even months since I'd last seen them, and a part of me wanted to keep walking until I got to our door, opened it up and said, *Hey, Daddy, your baby girl is home.* But it'd been a long time since I'd been his baby girl. A long time since I'd helped Jesse Jr. hold the garlic press up high, letting the juice drip down over a bowl of hot spaghetti till the whole house smelled like the promise of something good coming.

I felt myself starting to shake and kicked at the broken-down door on the House, hollering loud for T-Boom to open it.

There was smoke coming out of the chimney, so I knew he was inside. The old gray boards nailed to the windows flapped where wind pushed up underneath them, and even from way off there was the smell of something bitter burning.

I kicked at the door again, calling T-Boom's name so loud my throat hurt.

You lost your mind, girl? You want the police all over me?

He'd gotten skinnier over the months, and his hair was long, coming almost to his shoulders. The plaid shirt he was wearing had a hole in the arm. I used to love the way he looked in that shirt, the red and black squares of it, the way he'd pull the collar up when he was cold. Now I just stared hard at the hole, trying to find somewhere besides him to put my eyes.

You heard me calling you the first time. I know you did.

He held out his hand, and I put the money in it. Mostly quarters but some dollar bills, too. My stomach hurt from missing lunch, but I knew the moon would fill that hunger up quick.

T-Boom shivered, shaking a little as he counted the money. *You still out by Donnersville?*

I hugged myself, nodding. It'd become just this—me giving him the money, him giving me the moon and sometimes a few questions in between it all. No more T-Boom and Laurel. Cheerleader and Co-Captain. No more us together always.

Yeah, mostly. Still got that room back behind the hardware store. Nobody bother me there.

Nobody try to come in at night?

Uh-uh. Got something waiting for them if they do. My foot where they don't want it. No one's trying to get in there.

Donnersville meth heads cleaned it out a long time ago, T-Boom said. *Steal the shoes off their own mothers' feet for some moon. They don't care. Don't you become like them, Laurel. You're better than that.*

I just looked at him.

My mom said she saw your daddy at the Hy-Vee, T-Boom said. *Food shopping with little Jesse. Said Jesse's getting tall, don't sit in the cart anymore but was riding on the side of it.*

T-Boom put the money in his pocket and handed me two small bags—more than I had money for. He always gave me a little extra.

Long as I stay in Donnersville, he's not trying to get me. After the last time, Daddy said he's through with me. Jesse Jr. look like he eating? He never liked to eat. That's why I give him those vitamins. I stopped talking quick as I'd started. Jesse Jr. was my heart, and whenever there was room in my brain, he came to it, quick and fast as a storm. I reached into one of the bags T-Boom had just handed me, put a tiny bit of the moon on my tongue. It burned melting, then the burning was gone and there was the light, the moonlight. And for a minute, there wasn't Jesse Jr. or Daddy somewhere.

T-Boom shrugged. *He told my mama they were thinking about packing up,* he said. *Thinking about heading back to Pass Christian.*

He's been saying that since we left there. Always talking about going home. Like there's some "home" to go to.

I closed my hand tight around the bags and looked out over the land. Galilee was flat and cold. Real different from Pass Christian. When I was still living with Daddy and my brother, I'd put Vaseline on me and Jesse Jr.'s lips every morning, to keep them from chapping and bleeding. Now my own lips were too often cracking and bloodied. The moon soothed them, though. Soothed me. I tried not to wonder if Daddy was remembering about the Vaseline. Tried not to think about Jesse Jr.'s lips cracking in this cold. My hands shook as I put another little bit of it in my mouth, felt the burning. Then the light. I smiled because Galilee wasn't ugly and flat and cold anymore. It was somebody's promised land.

I pressed my hands together and held them to my chin, like I was praying, the tiny plastic bags of moon warm inside them. Closed my eyes against the voices and memories coming at me. *Hurricane Camille,* my daddy had said a long time ago. *Now, she was something to be afraid of. Came through the*

Pass in 1969 and just about took everything with her. But we came back, my daddy said.

The Pass always comes back. It was me and my daddy's voice saying it together. And for a minute, we were back in the Pass, sitting on the beach, the waves washing soft over our feet, the sun bright in our eyes. Daddy smiled, leaned back on his elbows and tilted his face toward the sun. Dark freckles spread across his nose and onto both cheeks. Angel kisses. So many angel kisses. He'd started growing a beard, and there was red in it. Gray too. I reached up and touched his face, amazed at how soft the hair was there. My daddy caught my hand in his and kissed it before letting go. He was telling me about the water, how it had always been there, bringing us everything we needed—food, jobs, hope. *It's never let us down, Laurel. The water's never let us down.*

You should go with them, Laur. You should go home.

I opened my eyes to T-Boom standing in front of me, the water gone. I didn't look at him, just stared hard at the House, trying to snatch those voices and that memory of me and Daddy from my head.

The Pass is gone, T-Boom. No place to go back to. My

daddy's just talking. Just saying words to say them.

Inside, T-Boom had a whole lot of candles burning, and the house seemed to be breathing with the light. I wondered again who lived here once. Whose old house this was before the boards got nailed to it and the lights got turned off. I'd found a deserted place too—a tiny back room in J. Turner's old hardware store. Had been staying there awhile. J. Turner died two years before, and his family was fighting over who inherited what. Either everybody wanted it or nobody wanted it, but in the meantime, they left it to collect dust. Water still flowed in the toilet, but no lights worked. No heat came on. Mostly it was dark and cold back there. Quiet as anything. Easy to get to by a small cellar door that had a broken lock on it. I'd gotten some police line tape and strung that across. Nobody tried to come in, and my guess is most people feared finding a body in there. Whatever the reason, I'd never woken up to find anybody standing over me.

This kid out in Donnersville said it's not good to have all those flames in the house with the moon cooking, I said.

T-Boom shrugged. *Those Donnersville meth heads*

don't know. Unless that kid's gonna come get the electric turned on, he needs to shut up. I know what I'm doing. Keep everything separate. T-Boom cursed and looked hard at me.

Sometimes the evil came fast to him—one minute smiling and the next, his face twisting into some kind of rage nobody saw coming. Once, on the basketball court, he knocked a kid from the other team clear across the gym. He was suspended for two games after that.

But most days, T-Boom was all sweetness, and it was hard not to remember that first time he walked over to me . . .

I felt the sadness creeping up quick, put another small taste of moon in my mouth and told T-Boom I had to go, that I'd see him next time.

You should think about going home, Laurel. I bet your daddy would take you back again. You just gotta leave the moon alone. Me and you, we're not like those meth heads—we could leave this stuff alone if we wanted to.

Yeah, I said. *I know that.*

But I knew all I was thinking about was how the

moon was washing over me, disappearing all the sadness.

T-Boom wiped his nose and sniffed hard.

I'm just about through with this, Laurel, he said. *There's a place up in Summitville I been hearing about, thinking about. Say they can clean you up real good, all the way so you don't slip back to wanting it. I know we don't need some program, but Coach said if I show him I could do it, I'd be back on the team come next season. Get two more years of playing in.*

He leaned against the doorway, swatting at some invisible something near his head. The moon did that, made you feel things that weren't there. *There's a place in Summitville,* he said again. *I'm gonna go there.*

Yeah, I said. *That sounds nice. That sounds real good. Summitville.*

They say it's easier if people do it together, T-Boom said. *Me and you could do it together. Then you could go back to cheering, and I could play ball again. Be like it used to be.*

I put my hands in my pockets and fingered the moon. The tiny plastic bags felt warm and good and right. Before I headed back out of town, I'd do a little bit more behind the 7-Eleven. Then walk for a while before trying to hitch back to Donnersville. With the moon inside of me, the walk wouldn't be cold, the night wouldn't be dark. I smiled at T-Boom. He was over six feet tall, but he looked small standing there twitching and swatting. He looked like something a little bit broken. Looked like some little kid's electric toy that was short-circuiting out.

It's all gonna be all right, T-Boom. We're all gonna be all right. I started walking backwards away from him. *No worries, T-Boom. We don't have any worries.*

T-Boom watched me. He said something, but I couldn't hear it. Then he stepped back, gave me a long, broken-faced look—like everything in the world that was wrong was his own fault—and closed the door.

other houses

AFTER I LEFT the House that night, snow started falling. It was early April, but snow was coming down. Not hard, just flakes of it, like tiny lights in the darkness. As I passed by window after window, I saw smiling families around dinner tables. It wasn't until I walked past the last window that I saw a woman carrying a ham to a table decorated with colored eggs and green plastic grass. I stopped then and stood there in the darkness watching the family bow their heads. It was Easter Sunday. A little boy turned in his chair and seemed to look straight at me. We stayed like that for I don't know how long—me looking into his life, him looking out at mine. Then the others raised their heads and he turned back toward the dinner. The moon was floating through me, and I smiled, thinking about Jesse Jr.—his face pressed against the car window, his eyes begging. Something warm and wet was surrounding me, and I laughed at the heat inside the snow. The hurt of wanting the moon was gone now, replaced by something heavy. Not heavy. Light. Free. I was free. Tears. The warm thing wasn't snow. Where were the tears coming from? Who was crying on me? I stopped walking and wiped at my eyes, but whoever was crying on me kept on crying. I laughed, and the tears came harder. Jesse Jr.'s face faded away, and Mama was there, laughing. Behind her, my grandmother, M'lady, sat on a porch, rocking slowly, looking at me like she couldn't quite see me. *Laurel?* She leaned forward and squinted into the darkness. *Is that you? Laurel . . . ?*

I walked faster, away from her. I didn't want her to see me with all of this water coming out of me. Didn't want her to be reminded.

Laurel.

I tried to run, but the hurting was back, and the cold was like a wall pushing against me.

Laurel!

I stopped—my breath coming heavy—and turned, ready to tell M'lady and Mama to go to Jackson. *It's dry in Jackson.*

Laurel, is that you?

Slowly, Mama faded, and M'lady turned into my friend Kaylee, shivering on her front porch. I looked around—how had I gotten on her street when Donnersville was in the other direction?

We stared at each other a long time. I could tell she was looking me over, taking in my ragged coat and bloody lips.

Laurel, she said, *look at you. Look at yourself! Who did you turn into?!*

pass christian, mississippi

THE CITY OF PASS CHRISTIAN sits right there on the Gulf of Mexico—blue-gray water and white sand so pretty my daddy used to say it reminded him of my mama's hair. Go down to the water, and the peace comes over you so deep you'd think it was the true ocean even if you'd never seen the sea. Hot wind damp with salt all day long until your skin freckled all over. If somebody would've told me that water and that sand and the way that wind blew my hair into my face wasn't always gonna be there, I would have looked at them and laughed and said what my daddy always used to say: *You ever met a person from the Pass that gave up when times got hard?*

In 2005 I was eleven years old, and I'd been in Pass Christian, right close to Long Beach, Mississippi, all my life. Since third grade, all I ever wanted to do was tell stories. I'd tell them to whoever was listening, and most times that person was the Grandlady of the House—my mama's mama. From the time I could talk, she'd said that's what I had to call her, not Grandma or Nana or even her name—Helene. The Grandlady of the House—or M'lady.

M'lady was tall and, as she always said, *thick boned, not fat. There's a difference, Laurel.* She had blue hair hanging long down her back, and I thought that blue was the prettiest color hair I'd ever seen. *It's the rinse I use,* she'd say to me. *This shade's hard to come by. You see people trying for it all the time, but most times, theirs is off-color, like dank water.*

Some days, I'd just climb up onto the couch and sit running my fingers through her hair. Felt like hours I could do that, us just sitting quiet, me running my fingers through her long blue hair.

She could make just about anything—pretty crocheted doll dresses, grits and boiled shrimp, sweet potato pie with a Louisiana praline crust. She'd been born in Louisiana, and there was French in her blood. And that's how she learned to make gumbo. *I don't just make any old gumbo,* M'lady would say, stirring so many things into the big pot so fast that I got dizzy from watching. *I make a gourmet gumbo. Not everybody can cook gourmet. They might say they can, but their cooking's just regular. Watch here, Laurel. Learn yourself some gourmet.* On the days she made gumbo, people always found a way to just drop by our house to talk about church or the weather or how fish didn't seem to be biting.

Anyone could be a grandma, Laurel, M'lady said to me one morning. *All you do is have yourself some children and wait for those children to have themselves some children and then it's done. But it takes more than that to be a Lady.*

We were sitting on her couch. The small hole I'd dug in it had some filling sticking out, and I pulled at it until M'lady slapped my hand away.

Not anybody, M'lady, I said. *Not daddies.*

Not men, I guess. M'lady was working the hem out of a pair of my pants. I'd grown over the winter, and it was springtime. When I pulled the pants on, they stopped just above my ankles, and M'lady bent down and raised up the hem, saying, *There's some fabric here. We could get another good inch out of these.*

I watched her work the seam ripper underneath the material, then gently slide it along until it hitched on something, making her slow down a bit to work through the thicker stitches.

And you can't be a grandma if you don't get old, I said, my fingers slowly finding their way back to the hole in the couch.

M'lady stopped working the pants and looked at me, her pale eyes almost the same color as her hair.

You planning not to get old?

Just last week you told me that some people just don't get old. Said some people die before they even get one baby going.

M'lady went back to the pants and made a *tsk* sound. *Since when do you listen to everything I say? And remember it, too.*

You told me I have to listen if I want to tell stories. Told me the best stories come from other people's stories. You don't remember saying that, M'lady?

Hmph, M'lady said. But she was smiling to herself.

She finished one leg and moved over to the other, gathering the cuff around her hand.

My plan is this—you gonna get old, Laurel. You gonna grow up first, though, find your husband—somebody you love a lot and loves you more—

I started to huff about not wanting a husband, but M'lady shushed me.

Just listen to me, girl. Just listen.

I folded my arms and threw myself back against her couch, but I didn't say anything more.

You gonna start writing down your stories. He's gonna listen to you read them, and he'll tell you everything he loves about them—just like I do now.

M'lady looked at me and smiled. I tried not to smile back, but I did a little bit.

Then you and your husband gonna have some babies. My great-grandbabies. I plan to be here to see at least one or two get born. And one day, they'll have some babies and you'll be old like me and you'll remember this talk. And you'll smile . . . remembering me.

I laid my head against M'lady's arm and didn't say anything. My mind on the future she'd already put down for me.

this storm coming

THAT DAY, I stopped just telling M'lady my stories and started writing them down. M'lady said as long as she was living, she'd make it her duty to keep me in little notebooks, took me to the office supply store in town and bought me four right on the spot. Pencils and pens and some dog-shaped erasers for the times I changed my mind about what I wanted to write. A few mornings later, I came running home to her, holding high up in the air a notebook filled with stories I'd written just that day.

Laurel, you do any listening in school or just all this writing? M'lady asked, flipping through the pages, trying real hard not to smile.

I did a little bit of listening, I said back. *But the teacher didn't say anything interesting to me. And the people in my stories, they just started talking louder.*

Then M'lady laughed hard, throwing her head back, blue hair flying. Strange how being able to make a person laugh fills you up with something good. *Lord, girl, you're something else.*

Late in the afternoon, after the hot Pass Christian sun went down, you could feel the breezes coming off the water. We'd head slow toward it, M'lady's dress blowing, always pale blue or gray or green. Always reminding me of the water.

We'd walk on Market until the sidewalks turned to sand, then we'd turn and head along West Beach, walking along the water.

Mississippi heat's hard to explain. Like walking out into thick steam some mornings and hard to move. But the afternoon I brought my first story home to M'lady, the weather had turned, the thick air heavy and wet, dark clouds hanging low over us as we walked.

They keep talking about this storm coming, M'lady said. She stopped walking, leaned hard on her cane and looked up at the sky. *Saying we need to be heading inland, find shelter.*

We got shelter, I said. *Our house.*

M'lady shook her head and started walking again. I could see the water now, the small waves higher than usual, white capped and angry-looking.

They said it's gonna be badder than a house can hold. Your daddy's taking y'all up Jackson tomorrow, stay with your cousins there and wait it out.

Not going to Jackson, I said. *They can go by themselves. I'm staying here with you, M'lady. Or you come with us if it's supposed to be bad like they're saying.*

M'lady shook her head again. *It's just talk, Laur. People need something to get people scared about. A storm's a storm, and I've waited out plenty of them. But your daddy's taking you and your mama and baby Jesse just in case, so you'll go. I'll be right here when y'all get back.*

We walked slow the rest of the way to the water. Stood at the edge of it a long time, watching it move toward us.

galilee sunrise

GALILEE SUNRISE IS LIKE NOTHING anybody could ever dream of, except God. I guess he decided to take the prettiest sunrise and put it down right here. When we first moved here, me, Daddy and Jesse Jr. would go to the sunrise service at Christ's House Church, and we'd get up real early. I'd have my clothes laid out on my bed so I just had to wash up and get in them. Then I'd sit brushing my hair while it was still near dark out. We'd wait to the very last minute to wake Jesse Jr. because once he was awake, nobody could do anything except make sure he didn't break something or break himself. I'd braid my hair down my back and wrap a colored elastic around the end. Daddy would be in the bathroom shaving and humming. Mostly he hummed Christian songs because that was mostly all he listened to.

Just a little while before we left, we'd get Jesse Jr. up, dress him and feed him something. Jesse Jr. shared a room with me, and his bed was in one corner, mine in the other. Aside from those two beds and a small rug, there wasn't much to our room. Wasn't much to our house. A couch and two chairs in the living room and a coffee table with a wobbly leg. A small TV connected up to a big satellite dish outside. Some pictures on the wall. A few pots and plates in the kitchen. We had a white tablecloth that I put out for birthdays and Thanksgiving. In the two closets in the living room, we had clothes—me and Jesse Jr.'s in one closet, Daddy's in the other. My daddy would say, *When our ship comes in, there won't be enough closet space in this house, so I guess we're gonna have to move to a mansion then.* Then we'd be all dressed heading out to the car with that pretty sunrise looking down over us. Those mornings, as we drove quiet to church, it felt like we'd been given a whole new life. It was different, but it was ours, and in it, we had just about everything we needed—we had each other and God and that beautiful Galilee.

daddy:
part one

I DID LEAVE THE MOON ALONE for a while. After Daddy found it under my pillow, he sat on the edge of my bed and cried.

It isn't mine, I said, turning away from him.

I hadn't seen him cry since the day we buried Mama and M'lady, and to see the tears coming that way—hard and fast, him taking big gulps like his breathing was gonna stop, made me take my own deep breaths and pray that the moon flowed out of me. Forever and ever. I didn't want to hurt my daddy like that. Never wanted to hurt my daddy.

Outside, a freezing rain was falling hard. Maybe it was a Saturday, but already I had mostly stopped going to school, so the days blurred over themselves with the only distinction being night breaking into day and day to night again.

Whose is it, then? And what the hell is it, anyway? Daddy opened the bag and sniffed it. He turned back to my pillow and flung it to the foot of my bed. There was a small metal pipe there, blackened at one end from the flame and the moon.

Oh, dear Laurel . . . dear God! my daddy said, closing his eyes tight like that could make everything disappear. *Dear God in Heaven help—*

Give it to me!

Daddy looked up, like he'd forgotten I was there, his tears still coming.

Give it to me! I whispered, my voice trembling. I had just come out of the shower, and my hair was wet and dripping, my back and legs still damp in my shorts and T-shirt.

You're not this, Laurel. Me and your mama and M'lady didn't make you this!

Just give it to me! I said again. I had been standing across the room from him, but now I moved fast toward him, hitting at him and trying to grab the moon. But my daddy was faster. Even though he was crying, he snatched the pipe and the moon away from me and with his other hand grabbed my arm so hard it hurt.

You're hurting me!

But he didn't let go.

Where did you get it, Laur?

It's Kaylee's! I was crying now, needing the moon that was so close . . . *Kaylee asked me to hold it for her!*

Does Donna know?

I didn't answer him.

Does Kaylee's mama know she's using this stuff, Laur? Answer me!

Give it to me! I was shivering now.

My daddy put the pipe and the moon in his pocket, then took my face in both of his hands, looking hard at me. His own face was red and wet from crying, and even as he held my head, the tears kept coming.

God help us, he whispered, dropping my face and turning away from me.

Give it to me!

But my daddy was walking out of my room. In another minute, I heard his car starting and then speeding down the road, my moon in his pocket, toward Kaylee's house.

I leaned against the wall and lowered myself down. My whole body trembled with wanting the moon. Jesse Jr. came in, dragging his stuffed bear behind him.

Don't cry, Laurel, he said, his tiny hand rubbing my back. *Mama's in heaven. Don't cry.*

Leave me alone for a little while, Jesse! I said.

But Jesse Jr. ignored me, his tiny hand moving in circles over my back, his voice soft in my ear. *Don't worry, Laurel. She's not scared anymore.*

water rising up

I USED TO WALK AND WALK after I ran away. Had to keep moving, had to let the moon move through my body, keep flowing, and didn't feel the heat on me till my skin burned. No rain hardly, but still if I stopped moving, the visions of the water came at me. I heard the crushing of rock against rock. Heard the Mississippi roaring. Couldn't breathe through all the water coming down and over me. There's my house . . . washing away. Water like somebody's angry hand slamming it to pieces.

And you'll smile, M'lady said. *Remembering me.*

Her voice inside my head over and over . . .

There's my friend Emmajean's daddy's Honda—

EJ's doll against the window as the car twisted through the water, landing topside down two hundred feet away.

There's the oak tree we used to climb, lying on its side now, five feet high. *Count the rings,* my science teacher said that year. *And it'll tell you the age of the tree.* How many hundreds of rings beneath that clump of dirt and roots? How deep is that hole the tree left behind?

EJ's daddy stayed behind. I hear her and her mama settled in Texas. What was the song me and Emmajean used to sing together? *Miss Sue. Bless You. Say it with an eye closed. Touch your head, shoulder, nose. Miss Sue . . .* Strange not to know anybody who remembers the words.

But we were already gone by the time the water rose up. We'd driven away at sunrise, the clouds low and dark, the gulf already angry and creeping high up, rain coming down. My daddy said, *The storm might pass right over,* and my mama looked at him. *Y'all getting out of here till it does, Charles. Come right back to me when it's passed on by.* And so we pulled into the long line of cars driving away from the water. Behind us, M'lady waved.

But you were coming with us, Mama.

I can't leave M'lady here, precious. And she's too stubborn to leave.

Then Mama touched my hair, pulled my braid to her lips and kissed it. *You be sure to brush your hair in the morning, you hear me? Keep it pretty.*

I reached through the car window and held on to her real hard.

If it gets bad, we'll go over to the Walmart, Mama said. *That's our plan. I don't want y'all worrying. Me and M'lady going to be fine.*

Big store like Walmart should be safe enough, M'lady said. *No storm coming through those heavy walls.* And to me she said, *I'll buy you something pretty.*

I'll buy you something pretty.

I'll buy you something pretty.

I'll buy you something pretty.

galilee

WE STAYED IN JACKSON for two years. Jesse Jr. learned to crawl in Aunt G.'s kitchen, took his first steps across Aunt G.'s sunporch floor, said Laur before he could say Daddy and called Aunt G. Mama the morning we packed up the car to head to Galilee.

As we stood in Aunt G.'s driveway, hugging our good-byes and wiping away tears, I wondered if this was the beginning of some new life for me—a life filled up with tears and good-byes and moving on to the next place.

We took Route 55 out of Jackson, then 80 all the way across. There was a job waiting for Daddy in Galilee. They'd even found a place for us to live there.

A small house outside of town, Daddy said. *I love your aunt G. like she's my own sister, but we need to be in our own home again, Laur. Need to be moving on.*

I sat up front with Daddy, stared at the flat land as we drove. Big sky that I couldn't look up into without thinking about M'lady and Mama. Green land moving fast toward us, then passing us by. Farms and fields. Whole stretches with nothing at all. I watched Mississippi grow small behind me. *Next time I see you, you'll be a lady,* my aunt said, hugging me hard. *Already look so much like your mama I can't hardly stand to look at you.* And then more tears.

We stopped for hamburgers somewhere. We slept in the car and washed up in a gas station. I woke up once, and we were in Iowa. Woke up again and it was near morning and we were here. Moving slow past a big blue sign that said

WELCOME TO GALILEE
WHERE LIFE IS A WALK ON WATER.

Sounds promising, my daddy said. *New place. New life. Put our past behind us.*

Jesse Jr. slept hard in his car seat behind me. I listened to the soft sound of the motor and my daddy's hand drumming against the steering wheel. On the radio, a deep-voiced man was talking about lamb and sheep, about Christ and blood. I stared up at the sky—blue and cloudless. The morning we had the service for M'lady and Mama, my daddy took my hand, pointed up at the same blue and cloudless sky. *That's where they are now,* he said. *Safe. Closer to God. Water's never gonna rise that high.*

We drove slow down the main street—past a grocery store and a secondhand shop. A flower store with its gray gates pulled halfway down and a bucket of wilted daisies out front. I rolled down my window and let the warm air come over me. A group of teenagers was hanging out in front of a 7-Eleven, and as we drove past, they looked at me and I looked back at them. They looked different from my friends in Pass Christian—dark haired and pale skinned, like the sun wasn't on them year round. I put my hand on my own face, knowing the color was already leaving it, my freckles fading, the sun's heat on it feeling like something from a long time ago. We looked at each other, and I tried not to think about my Pass Christian friends—scattered all over and none of us knowing where the others were. Tried not to think about us together in the school yard, at the beach, walking to get ice cream. Just a group of kids going somewhere, that's all we were. Like something real normal, real *always*.

After a few minutes, I rolled the window up again and lay back against my seat. Galilee looked like a whole lot of other towns we'd been through—flat and small and landlocked.

You okay, baby girl? my daddy asked. He put his hand on my leg, then patted it quick and put it back on the steering wheel. *How okay can I be?* I wanted to scream. *My whole life got washed away.*

But my daddy looked so hopeful, so ready to make this new place work for us.

Yeah, I said. *My life is a walk on water.*

daddy:
part two

WHEN MY DADDY came into my room that night after talking to Kaylee's mom, Donna, he hugged me real hard without saying anything for a long time.

Jesse Jr. was asleep on the other side of the room. I'd made him eggs and sliced ham for dinner, a few boiled carrots with brown sugar on them for his vegetable. *Why you shaking, Laurel?* Jesse'd asked me. *You cold? You want my blanket?*

I could hear his breathing coming slow and calm. Jesse Jr. always slept deep after he ate, his mouth a little bit open, his hand clutching tight to his blanket.

My daddy pulled a chair in from the kitchen up to the side of my bed.

We're gonna move through this, Laurel, he whispered. *We got through everything else. This is gonna be easy as pie.*

Then he started crying again. I stared out the window at the rain and darkness, tried to slip my mind out of the room, away from him crying, away from the hurting coming on inside me.

He stayed in my room all night—rubbing my back as I jerked myself in and out of sleep. Praying. At one point, I screamed and swung at him in the darkness, but he just caught my hand and gently held it until I was asleep again.

Dear Heavenly Father—We don't ask for the return of loved ones that you've taken to your Upper Room, I woke to hear him whispering. *But please let me hold on to Laurel—full-on. Please don't take her too, dear Lord.*

I slept through the next day. And most of the day after that.

My daddy came into my room each morning and set a tray of food beside my bed—toast and jam at breakfast time, with orange juice in the Elmo cup we'd found in the back of the car on our way out of

Pass Christian. It'd been mine when I was little, and maybe I'd left it in the car at some point, so that when it rolled from under the seat, me and Daddy both smiled, remembering.

But all day long, the cup sat there with the orange juice getting warm inside it.

On the morning of the third day, my whole body felt like someone was dipping me into ice water and leaving me in there only long enough to feel the pain—then pulling me out again. Even my brain hurt, but when I tried to cry, no tears came—just deep hunger for the moon.

When I came into the kitchen that morning, Jesse Jr. was sitting at the table eating a bowl of cereal, milk dripping from his chin. Daddy was sitting across from him, reading the Bible and drinking coffee. When he saw me, he smiled, like every prayer he'd ever spoken had been answered. I stared at him. There were deep rings beneath his eyes.

I leaned back against the kitchen wall and closed my eyes, the pain behind them like a knife. Every part of my body itched. I couldn't scratch any one place hard or long enough.

You see I don't need that stuff, Daddy, I said, scratching hard at my legs. *I only did it once. I was just seeing what it was like. I'm okay now. I'm all right . . .*

kaylee before

WE HAD BEEN LIVING IN GALILEE for two days when Kaylee showed up at our front porch. I'd never seen hair like hers—dark and curling perfectly down over her shoulders. Her skin was different, too—dark like she'd been in the sun all her life—but without freckling or burning or paling up in the wintertime.

The night before, it had rained—a soft light rain that smelled like heat. The rain was different from Pass Christian rain—no salt in it. No sea air. Different from Jackson, too. The next morning, the rain was gone, and when I walked out onto the porch, I was struck near dumb by how bright green the tree leaves were. All along the street, the leaves stood out that way so that when Kaylee walked up to our porch that morning, there I was, sitting and staring at the tree leaves like I was seeing them for the first time—wondering how all that color could be in them that way.

You write? Kaylee asked.

I looked down at the notebook I had left open on my lap—the blank page just sitting there like it was laughing at me.

I shrugged.

I wish I could write, she said. *I like to read, though. If you need a reader, I'm that person. A hundred and ten books in my house and counting. I read all of them. Some sucked, but I kept reading, hoping they'd turn good at some point. They didn't, though. But you don't just give up on something—*

She stopped talking as quickly as she'd started. One minute, the words were pouring out of her, then nothing.

I closed my notebook. And for a long time, neither one of us said anything.

Then Kaylee told me her name.

Maybe I told her mine. I must have. I must have said, *I'm Laurel Daneau. We just moved here from Pass Christian.* Or maybe I said *from Jackson*—or maybe I didn't—like Jackson was a sidestep, a quick stop on our way to Galilee. Like Jackson wasn't two years and three cousins and a house too small for all of us together. Pass Christian was my somewhere before this. I didn't want to erase Jackson. I just wanted to hold on to Pass Christian. Hold on hard to it.

But the next thing Kaylee said to me made me stop cold and put my head down, my forehead pressing hard against my notebook.

I know. I know all about the flood and your mama and grandma. I came by to say I'm sorry.

We stayed there like that—me with my head down, taking deep breaths. Kaylee standing in front of me, her hands in her pockets.

I'm sorry.

Wasn't your fault. You didn't bring the water. There was a meanness to my words that I hadn't expected to come out of me. But I didn't want some strange girl feeling sorry for me. Our whole two years in Jackson had been filled up with people I didn't even know coming up to us all sad-eyed and sorry. I didn't want to be pitiful here in Galilee. Didn't want the looks, the nosy questions, the creepy desire for my family's Oh-So-Sad story.

I know. I just wish none of it ever happened, and I'm sorry it did. That's all.

When I looked up, Kaylee was staring at me and holding out a handful of Hershey's Kisses.

Supposedly, something about chocolate is good for sadness, she said. *I read that somewhere.* Then she smiled at me.

I must have smiled back, because Kaylee sat down beside me on the porch. In my memory, it's the first time I'd smiled in a long time. And Kaylee must have somehow known that, because she told me my smile was like a light getting turned on. I'd never heard anything like that before. *A light getting turned on.*

Maybe you can write it into the past, and that will help leave some of it there. People do that. They write stuff down and then it's gone from them and they're free.

How do you know that? I thought you said you didn't write.

I don't, Kaylee said. *I read—like I told you. You put it in front of me, I'm gonna read it. And somebody must've put a book about writing in front of me at some point, because I remember that part—about writing away the past. I remember thinking, "That must be like magic." Like having a giant Memory Eraser. How cool is that? Anything embarrassing or really hard or really painful—boom! Gone. Until you get the guts to pick up what you wrote and reread it—*

She stopped talking again. Felt like she was in the middle of a sentence and just closed her mouth.

Why do you do that? I asked her.

Do what?

Stop talking like that.

Kaylee shrugged. After a little while passed, she said, *I don't want to talk too much, that's all. They're your memories . . . to do with whatever you want. I shouldn't be sitting here trying to tell you where to put them. That's all.*

I didn't think that's what you were trying to do. I liked what you were saying.

I looked out over Galilee and squinted against the sunlight. Where the leaves tried to block it out, it snuck in around them and made pretty yellow lines along the road. I peeled the silver foil away from a Hershey's Kiss and let the chocolate melt down over my tongue.

Galilee's a good place to make some new friends, Kaylee said.

I thought about the kids I'd seen the first time Daddy drove into town—how different they'd looked from my Pass Christian friends.

Kaylee was taller than me, and sitting beside her, I had to look up a little bit to see her eyes. They were pretty—brown with little bits of green jumping through, like some kind of light was jumping out of her.

You ever lived anywhere else? I asked her.

Yeah—when I was a baby, we lived in Colorado, but I don't remember. My mama got a picture of me by some mountains—that's pretty much the only proof I got of living there. Guess that's why I like reading so much—can just leave this place if I want to and don't even have to get on a bus or plane to go.

You got a lot of friends here? I asked. Maybe because I wanted to be her only friend. Maybe because I was afraid she could just disappear into all her friends and leave me standing.

But Kaylee shook her head. *I cheer. I got people who cheer with me. But since we're so far from town, mostly, aside from cheering, I stay home. People call this part of Galilee the country. Not like Galilee's that big, but where we are is still far away from everything.*

Cheering? I asked. *Like a cheerleader?*

Kaylee nodded. *There's tryouts at the end of the month—for next season. I bet you'd make the team easy.*

You think?

Kaylee smiled. *Yeah. All you need is a big mouth—the routines come easy.*

This big enough? I opened my mouth wide, and Kaylee laughed.

Looks big enough to me. Least big as mine.

Good. Then I guess I'll be trying out.

After that, we just sat there smiling, staring out at nothing. Galilee's a quiet town—just farms out by us. In town, there's just a Walmart, a Payless, a Dollar Store, and the supermarket. Once you pass those, you're not in Galilee anymore, and the road you're on turns into highway, taking you west toward Colorado and Wyoming and east toward Illinois and Ohio. Me and Kaylee watched a car drive down the street, listened to the sound of a train whistle blowing far off.

I'm not staying out here in the country past high school, Kaylee said. *You can come with me if you want. Maybe California. Or Texas. Someplace big and far away.* She looked at me. *If we end up being friends, I mean.*

M'lady used to ask me, *Who will stand beside you with the Lord?* For a long time I didn't know what she was talking about, and I used to say, *Angels.*

Of course angels. But who else? Who will stand beside you, Laurel?

The last time she asked, we were sitting on a bench by the water. The sun was dark red, and no wind was blowing. Late afternoon, and soon Mama would cash out her drawer at the Dollar Store, pull off her apron, rub her growing belly and punch the clock. Then she'd say good-bye to those staying for the late shift and head down to the water to meet us. The three of us would sit for a while, sharing the candy bars Mama'd brought us, making dinner plans and watching the fishing boats come in and go out. These were our days in the Pass—slow that way and unsurprising.

And while we waited for Mama to come, me and M'lady talked. And talked.

While you're living, M'lady said. *It's the Rocks in your life that will stand beside you. Your words, your friends. Your family.*

How many Rocks does a person get, M'lady?

M'lady put her hand on my thigh and smiled out at the water, her hair a long blue braid down her back.

If you're lucky, she said, *you get as many as you need.*

As me and Kaylee sat there, letting the chocolate melt in our mouths and staring out at nothing, I let the thoughts of M'lady move over me, slow and calming as a breeze. It'd been a long time since I'd felt anything but sadness when I thought of her, and sitting there with the sun coming down, with Kaylee all new and promising beside me, I felt like M'lady was right close somewhere, taking every little bit in . . . and smiling.

Texas, I said to Kaylee. *I bet we'd like it there.*

t-boom

I MADE THE SQUAD EASILY. Maybe because I'd spent the two years before in Aunt G.'s yard, doing cartwheels and back bends, walk overs and round-offs. Some mornings, Aunt G. came outside to find me hanging from my cousins' jungle gym—just hanging there, my mind miles and miles away. *Oh, my stars, Laurel,* she'd say. *We need to get you into some gymnastics.* But it didn't happen. We were always leaving Jackson but never gone from there. Jobs turned up for Daddy in other places. Then they fell through. Friends promised work on fishing boats, then there wasn't work. Again and again, the hope rising, then falling. Rising and falling so that our small bags remained half packed, our toiletries remained travel size. Me and Jesse Jr. outgrew our clothes—he got my cousins' old stuff, I picked out things from the Salvation Army. And the days passed with me twirling around Aunt G.'s yard, maybe thinking if I hung long enough, spun fast enough, flipped high enough, the image of water pouring over Pass Christian would erase itself, melt into the spinning inside my head and disappear. It never did.

Then I was in Galilee, spinning in front of a long line of girls, cartwheeling and back-flipping and throwing my hands into the air until the captain of the squad said, *Well, duh! Hell yes on you!* And just like that, I was a Tiger, dressed in black and orange, running out onto the basketball court behind Kaylee, my pom-poms high in the air.

And always, always, there is Kaylee—my reader, my neighbor, my best friend—close to me.

Stop, look and listen! We are the mighty Tigers!

Stop, look and listen! We are the mighty Tigers!

Stop!

And then T-Boom is running onto the court, number twenty-three, eleventh-grade co-captain.

Give us some more of that Boom-Boom!

T-Boom with his hands up, high-fiving the other players as he runs through the double line of them.

His arms are long and pale. When he gets close to me, I see there's a dark blue bowl tattooed on the left one and below that bowl, in thick letters, the word *gumbo*. Gumbo like a dream coming toward me.

Who will stand beside you, Laurel?

Then I'm in M'lady's kitchen, Pass Christian heat thick around us and the pot bubbling, steam rising from it, the smell of it so *now,* so right here. *T-Boom, take me home . . .*

Time stops here.

The crowd is loud but then it's not. The people are all around us and then they're not—just me and T-Boom, with no sound, no people, between us. Just me and T-Boom, seeing each other—not for the first time, really, but, yes, for the first time. Because all those times before this night, all through the fall and early winter, he was just another guy on the team, just Boom-Boom, Number Twenty-Three, taking foul shots from the line, dribbling the ball down the court. Before, he was just jump shots and layups, laughing with his teammates while we practiced cheer after cheer after cheer.

T-Boom, please take me home . . .

And then the crowd is back, like a loud wind blowing around me. *Stop, look and listen!* We're yelling and we're stomping and clapping and throwing our pom-poms in the air and remembering to smile, but there is that word, and there is T-Boom, circling around me. *Stop!*

I think he likes you, Kaylee whispers each time T-Boom looks my way. He's home to me, and I don't even know him. He's salt sea air and hot sand. He's good things in a bowl and memory.

laurel

YOU'RE THE NEW ONE, *aren't you?* T-Boom asked me. *You coming with us over to the 7-Eleven?*

We had just won against Donnersville, and me and the other cheerleaders were walking out of the gym beside the basketball players. Kaylee's mother was going to pick us up later, and I was sleeping over at her house. Kaylee's eyes got big, and she nudged me, whispered, *I told you he likes you! Say yes!* So I said, *Yeah.* What else did I know that night but "yeah" for anything T-Boom wanted, anything he asked.

You like to party? he asked.

Yeah.

And there it was, my cheeks burning up, T-Boom smiling down at me, the excitement coming from everywhere.

A counselor at Second Chances said, *Go backwards in your life. Start from the place before the first time you ever saw the moon.*

Stop!

And I'm smiling now as Kaylee pulls my ponytail. *It's that blond hair,* she whispers. *Boys go crazy for blondes.*

But it's more white than blond. White like my mother's and maybe M'lady's before hers became blue. So white that people ask again and again, *Is that your natural hair color?*

Black and orange pom-poms bouncing against our legs as we run out of the gym—*We are the mighty Tigers!*

And when I look back, Jesse Jr. and my daddy are still in the stands, blowing me good-bye kisses. *We'll see you tomorrow* and two thumbs up from my daddy, his grin wide. *Good job, Laur!*

Good job, Laur, Jesse Jr. echoes, sticking his tiny thumbs up into the air.

Go backwards, the counselor said. *And don't stop when it gets painful. Don't stop when it gets hard.*

T-Boom. Co-Captain Cutie wants you! Kaylee says. *Crazy, huh?* But there is a longing in her voice—her whole life in Galilee, two years on this team, and here I come. *Still wet behind the ears,* M'lady would say. And the co-captain of the b-ball team wants to know if I like to party.

Yeah, I like to party!

Behind the 7-Eleven, plowed snow was piled high, with more snow coming down on top of it. T-Boom smelled like sweat and cold and a whole lot of familiar things. Smelled like someone I'd known forever. And me finally finding my words, finally finding the question I'd been wanting to ask.

How come you have that gumbo tattoo . . . ?

T-Boom laughed. His laugh was sweet, like somebody younger, somebody surprised by their own laughter.

I'm all mixed up, he said. *I'm always all mixed up. Just like the crazy-good gumbo my Louisiana grandma makes.*

And the word sounded like a song. *Louisiana.*

Maybe he played with my hair, shaking snow from it, pulling it out from where I'd tucked it inside my coat. *It'll get all wet,* I said. *Don't.* But I didn't want his hand moving too far away from me, so I let the word come quiet, fade quick as it left my mouth.

He kissed me. And his lips were soft and warm and familiar, familiar like this wasn't my first kiss but my hundredth kiss, my hundredth T-Boom kiss. But it wasn't. It was my first kiss, spinning inside gumbo and T-Boom and the sound of cheers echoing off the hardwood bleachers and snow whirling around me.

He said, *I hear you come from Mississippi. How'd you get so far from home?*

I just did, I said. *I just dropped from the sky.*

Well, I guess I'm lucky if girls like you just be dropping down from the sky.

The sky was gray where I dropped from. Then it was black. Then the land beneath my feet was gone. I didn't say this. Didn't tell T-Boom about my before life.

What else does your Louisiana grandma make?

Everything. You sound just like her. Slow-talking Southern drawl. He touched my hair again. *I could marry you in a minute.*

My face was hot, and the snow falling on it melted quickly. M'lady's voice shot into my head. *Find your husband—somebody you love a lot and loves you more . . .*

You all right, Laurel?

Yeah.

T-Boom pulled me to him again. He didn't try to kiss me again, just held me like that, close to his body, until M'lady's voice faded away and warm air crept up where the cold had been. I breathed deep into his coat and closed my eyes. I could hear Kaylee and some of the other girls laughing on the other side of the 7-Eleven. Way far off, I could hear the train moving through—going on through Missouri to get people down to Louisiana.

T-Boom pulled back away from me and took something out of his coat pocket.

You shivering like crazy, he said.

I looked closer at the clear plastic bag T-Boom was holding. There was something in it that looked

like powder that seemed to be glowing in the moonlight. For a moment, I just stood there next to him,
staring at that little piece of moon in his hand.
Then he rubbed the bag back and forth with his fingers some more, opened it, took a little bit out and
sniffed it off his finger. I watched the powder disappear inside T-Boom's nose. He closed his eyes, let
his head fall back and smiled.

What is that?

T-Boom opened his eyes slowly and looked at me.

What's that you got, T-Boom?

Then he looked at me a minute longer before
holding it out. *Something that's gonna take all that
shivering far, far away.*

galilee moon

THE FIRST TIME T-Boom held the moon to my nose, his fingers were warm and shaking. He touched one to his tongue, then dipped it into the bag and held it up for me. Seems slow motion, remembering now the way I moved my head down so that my nostril was right over that little bit of moon. The way T-Boom whispered *sniff hard,* and so I did, feeling something bitter drip down the back of my throat and then my head filling up with so many different beautiful things that I had to lean back against the 7-Eleven wall and let it drop down. I could feel the air on my teeth. Could feel something that must have been heaven moving through my body so fast and slow at the same time that I didn't know if I wanted to laugh real loud or cry or just let T-Boom move closer to me, lean in and add his kisses to all the beautiful other things. Then the whole world was moving fast in front of me and I jumped up high, did a quick flip in the air and laughed.

T-Boom watched me, smiling like he'd seen this a hundred times before. *You feel good, don't you?*

And I did. I felt great.

I felt like I was holding up the whole world and there was no water anywhere, no roads in front and behind me filled with empty land and tore-up houses. No past. Just this new, just this amazing, just this forever *now*.

Later on, when Kaylee came back behind there to get me, she said, *My mom's here, Laurel. We gotta go.* And I realized then my fingers were near blue from cold I didn't even feel. I looked hard at Kaylee—trying to see her clear, but she was wavy, standing right there but with all these shadows swaying around her.

You look wild-eyed. Was it that good? Kaylee

whispered as we started walking away. But I wasn't listening to her anymore. I was thinking about T-Boom and the moon and how I'd never known a person could feel a whole lot of things all at once that way and how glad I was we'd moved to Galilee because if it wasn't for this town, how would I have ever met T-Boom?

We got in Kaylee's mom's car that was all warm and humming. I put my head on Kaylee's shoulder and whispered, *I think I love him.* And maybe Kaylee laughed. Or maybe she just got quiet and stared out into the darkness.

happiness

LATE THAT NIGHT, and me and Kaylee sitting in her living room, the TV on but turned down—popcorn between us. Me not sitting so much as moving around and trying to be still, but how could I? How could I ever be still again?

Kaylee said, *Why are you so fidgety?*

I pressed my feet hard against the floor. Pressed my hands hard against each other, sat on the edge of the couch, felt the tingling running through me, making me want to jump.

T-Boom likes me! I just spent a whole hour making out with him! You'd be jumping out of your skin, too.

Can he kiss?

I couldn't stop nodding and smiling. My lips hurt. Maybe from the kissing. Maybe from the smiling. Maybe from the burn of the moon, I didn't know, but whatever it was, I didn't want it to ever stop.

Kaylee smiled. Her teeth were straight and white. With her dark and curly hair, she was so beautiful. She turned back toward the TV, twisting her curls around each other with one hand. A movie was on. A couple was dancing in it. The man held the woman in his arms. I thought about T-Boom.

My leg started to shake on its own. I tried to press it hard into the floor, but it wouldn't stop. Kaylee was looking at the TV and maybe talking about the game, but my mind was whirling. I got up again and started walking. If I had my way, I'd walk all the way back to T-Boom and his little square of moon.

I walked from one end of the living room to the other. There was a painting of Kaylee hanging on the wall above a small table. She was little in the picture. Wearing a pink and purple dress. Her hair was in braids with a million ribbons tied at the end. I tried to wrap my mind around being still enough to tie all those ribbons and couldn't.

I did the steps back across the room, trying to

touch her ceiling with each jump. *We are the mighty Tigers!*

I pulled at one of Kaylee's curls and watched it spring back. I jumped around her, singing, *I kissed him, I kissed him, I kissed that cute co-captain* to the tune of "A-Tisket, A-Tasket."

Kaylee laughed. *I used to love when my mom sang that song to me*, she said. *The real version, not your crazy made-up thing. I always wanted a green-and-yellow basket, and I always got so mad when that boy took her love letter.* She started singing, *I wrote a letter to my love and on the way I dropped it. I dropped it. I dropped it. On the way I dropped it. A little boy picked it up and put it in his pocket.*

Kaylee's singing voice was sweet and shy. I listened to her, trying to remember what songs my mother used to sing. None came to me, and I all of a sudden wanted Kaylee to stop singing, stop making me remember that I couldn't remember.

I like my version better, I said. *That singer's trying to force it to rhyme. Even a little kid could do that. I'm just a better songwriter, that's all.* I pulled her up. *Let's put on some music.*

Kaylee and I danced hard around her living room,

and the moving and singing loud felt so perfect, so right. I didn't want to ever stop.

Look at you, Laurel, Kaylee said. *You're happy. I like the way happy looks on you.*

She took my hand and spun me a bunch of times. Then did a high kick and sent the popcorn flying. For days and days, we laughed about that.

making
the moon

USED TO BE YOU *could make it easy,* T-Boom explained to me, his eyes bright, his arm around my shoulder, dark and warm inside his car, the moon moving through us making the world beautiful and bright. *Go to Walgreens and get your decongestant . . . get everything you need.*

T-Boom's arm tightening around my shoulder. No love like this since Mama, and since M'lady's arm around my shoulder saying, *Laurel, one day you're gonna . . .* but no! No more. No Pass Christian or Jackson . . .

Just the bright beauty, just T-Boom, his arm and the moon. Deep breath, and everything else is gone again. Deep breath and another sniff from T-Boom's beautiful finger.

They lock it all up now, though. They make you come in with a license. Stupid meth heads messed it up for everybody.

You can make this, T-Boom?

Yup. Got a runner—guy over in Gaston. His dad's a doctor. Gets me what I need most of the time. I found a house not too far from here. Like my own little laboratory. It's gonna make me rich.

I thought you said you're all mixed up. Don't sound mixed up to me. Sounds like somebody with all kinds of big plans.

I moved closer to him, closed my eyes when he kissed me. The sun was starting to go down, and we were parked behind school. I'd told my daddy I had cheering practice, and he'd smiled, said he'd take Jesse Jr. for pizza and maybe they'd save me some. There were other cars parked around us. The lights at the top of the flagpole had just come on and were shining bright, lighting up the track. I felt like I could run a whole mile around it and keep on going. Go so fast and so far . . .

All I ever think about, T-Boom said, *is living happily ever after.* He laughed. It was a sad, embarrassed laugh. *Can't believe I'm even saying that to anybody.*

I'm not anybody.

T-Boom looked at me. *I know. That's why I know I can say it to you.*

If somebody would have said *Imagine perfection, Laurel,* I would have imagined us just this way, with the track like a promise of something better. You just had to keep chasing it, keep dreaming it. I would have imagined the inside of T-Boom's car and me and him and the silence. And somewhere Mama and M'lady, talking soft and waiting for me to come home. I would have imagined a night exactly like this one, only with them living. A night where the present was the same. But the past was different.

stop, look
and listen

WE *WERE* THE MIGHTY TIGERS—people called us Galilee's Golden—and when me and Kaylee and all the cheerleaders ran out onto the floor, seemed everyone in Galilee was crowded into that gym and screaming for us. There was my daddy and Jesse Jr. sitting high up, their lumber-jack shirts buttoned tight against the Galilee cold. There was T-Boom's mama, small and fierce, with her bright red hair. And Kaylee's mama, Donna— smiling a grown-up Kaylee smile, calling to each of us, *Go Kaylee, Go Laurel, Go Brittany* . . . until each of us had a name for what seemed like the whole world to hear. Every game people telling us, *You* *are the mighty Tigers,* telling us, *Nobody's ever gonna stop y'all,* telling us we were already bigger and better and stronger than anything, so how could we not be the promise? *You are my promise,* my daddy said. *You got a whole world in front of you for you to take hold of. Anything you want is yours. Anything.* We *were* the mighty Tigers, and no one was ever gonna hold us down.

Thing about the moon is—it takes you deeper. Deeper than you'd go on your own.

The game over. Our fans gone home. Kaylee driving off with her mom but not before saying to me, *I thought you were sleeping over tonight.* And me promising next time.

You say that a lot these days, Laurel.

Don't be that way, K. You know T-Boom and me don't get to spend a lot of time this way.

Yeah. Kaylee rolling up her window and turning away from me. *That way.*

thunderation

THE CHEER BEGINS with one girl shouting, *Thunder!* and then the rest of us answer, *Thunderation!*

Then together we say,

We're the best team in the Nation.

What do we fight for?

Domination!

We're a winning

Generation!

Our team is Dynamite, and we're gonna win tonight, so sound off! Sound off! . . .

For some reason, this is the cheer I remember staying with me.

It goes on. More words. More steps. Someone

gets up on someone's shoulders, then flips down, turns, splits. Then we all split. And maybe this is why I remember it. The cheer ends this way—the way me and T-Boom did, the way me and Kaylee did, the way me and my daddy did—ends with the splitting. With all of us splitting.

And the bone-cold silence that follows the thunder.

confrontation

YOU SEEM DIFFERENT, Kaylee said to me one night when I actually did make it back to her house. Maybe a month had passed since T-Boom had first shown me the moon. Kaylee and I were sitting on her bed, but I was twitching to be back with T-Boom, and my head was throbbing.

I was annoyed at Kaylee. What did she know about anything? She'd never kissed anyone, had never felt someone like T-Boom holding her, had never known the moon.

I'm just me, I said. *Just the same old Laurel.* But I wasn't the same. I was different now. Better. Bigger. Stronger. Everything in the world felt more clear to me. T-Boom was mine, and we had some-thing—something good and real, bigger than the moon and the gumbo tattoo—me and T-Boom, we were together, connected in a way the rest of the world wouldn't ever be able to understand. Nobody got us, and that was all right because we had each other. *You know me like nobody's ever gonna know me,* T-Boom said to me one night. *You're inside me.*

And the moon was our secret from the rest of the world. The way the moon lifted us up and took us places nobody else could ever go to . . . how could Kaylee ever understand that? She was just a girl. Just somebody from Galilee who didn't know what it meant to go from Pass Christian to Jackson to here. Galilee was her always. And now I had an al-ways too—T-Boom.

It's like a part of you isn't even here anymore, Laurel.

You said you liked me this way. Liked me happy.

I do like you happy, but . . . something's off. It's either crazy happy or spaced-out or mad at me! And I don't even know what's coming when.

Kaylee's room was painted pale yellow. Striped curtains hung at the one large window that looked out over her family's fields. It was dark out, moonless.

I pulled the curtain back and stared out at it, imagining T-Boom appearing out in that darkness, like a ghost knight on a horse, come to rescue me.

People think you're doing meth, Laurel, I heard Kaylee say. I watched the ghost knight that was T-Boom come closer, lift his sword high into the air.

So much of it here. So many people doing it now. But I told them you weren't. Told them, given all that happened to you before you got here, they can't expect you to just be—

Kaylee stopped talking.

I let the curtain drop and looked at her. She was sitting across from me on the bed, her head down. She glanced up at me, then quickly back down again.

Are you, Laurel?

Am I what?

Are you doing meth?

Why would you even ask me that, Kaylee? Why would you even think I'm some meth head? Do I look like I'm doing meth?

I don't know. I don't know what it looks like . . . up close. I just want to know. So I could . . . I could help you, Laurel.

I got off her bed and started putting my coat on.

We were supposed to be having a sleepover, but I was done with her. She didn't know anything. Not about me. Not about anyone.

You sit in your perfect room with your perfect curtains and try to judge people, I said. *I don't need your help, Kaylee. I don't need you. And I don't care what people are saying.*

Laurel—Kaylee reached for my wrist, but I snatched it away—*I'm not judging you. Don't be like that*—

Yes you are. You all are. I see the way the squad looks at me. I see them whispering—

Laurel, we're friends . . . I'm asking—*I want to hear it from you. The truth . . . from you.*

I had my coat on and my bag on my shoulder.

No, I said, heading for the door. *I'm not a meth head. Happy, Kaylee? Does that answer your question?*

C'mon, Laurel. Don't be like this—

And then I walked out her door.

kaylee after

I WASN'T THERE when Daddy rang Kaylee's bell, but I could imagine it. Her mama answering it fast before it started the dog off barking and my daddy standing there, his head down, his eyes thick with tears. *I have some bad news, Donna,* then holding out his hand to show Donna the pipe, the moon.

I wasn't there, but I am now—inside this memory of it—Kaylee listening from behind her bedroom door, knowing it all now—where the moon came from, how I was going to go from sniffing to smoking, how I would move away from her—further and further until the afternoon she'd open her door to find me there, asking her for money. *I'll get it back to you, Kaylee. You know I'm good for it.* Her hand in the corner of her top right drawer where she kept the money she'd been saving—a month's worth of moon. *Take it, Laurel. Take it and leave me alone.* And me shaking, moon sick and ready to run.

The dream of Texas a long way behind us. A shadow of two girls on my front porch, the sun on us, the future filled up with promises it couldn't ever keep.

You my girl, Kaylee. You'll always be my girl.

I don't even know you anymore, Laurel. And Kaylee closing the door.

It's not mine, Mama, Kaylee said, stepping from behind the door, looking her mother in the eye in a way I had long ago learned not to do.

I know, Donna said, pulling Kaylee close to her. Because how could she have said to my father, *How could you not have known? How could you not have seen your daughter wasting away in front of you? Your daughter's darting eyes, her broken-out face, the tiny burns on her lips and fingers?* Donna hugging her daughter to her, not saying what she wanted to say—how she slowed down in front of our house, wanting to ring our bell, wanting to tell my father what she knew, what her daughter had cried into her lap after a game. *Laurel's doing meth, Mama. She's doing meth!*

And my daddy standing there, my pipe and moon in his hands, then turning, turning away from them and throwing it hard into the darkness.

I wasn't there. I was already mostly gone.

after t-boom

MY DADDY KEPT ME HOME from school for a week after he found my moon. And for a whole week, I didn't see T-Boom. *I drop it sometimes,* T-Boom had said to me way early on. *Just little bits of it around my room. If I wake up in the night needing some and there isn't a little bit close by, I just get down on the floor and look for the crumbs of it.* So I prayed I'd dropped the moon, knowing I hadn't, but still I crawled around my bedroom floor, picking up crumbs and hoping they were the moon. But mostly I slept, my body weak and sore, my skin itching everywhere at once.

Then it was Monday morning and I was standing

in the kitchen, the house empty, my daddy gone
back to work. A note on the table. *Food in the fridge.*
Please eat something. Love, Daddy & Jesse Jr.

The sun was bright as I stepped outside, dressed
for school—but I walked the other way, to the
House. To T-Boom.

People came around my mother's house sniffing, he
said.

I just need a little bit of the moon.

What'd you tell Kaylee's mother?

Nothing. I just want some moon, T-Boom.

*I can't have you coming around here, 'cause if you
freak out, then everybody freaks out.*

Just a little bit of the moon.

And it's not free all the time, Laurel . . .

*Just the moon, please, T-Boom. I can pay for it. Quit
talking. My skin hurts . . . !*

*You make me so mad, Laurel. This didn't have to get
all crazy. You didn't have to open up your big mouth.
What's with girls always blowing my cover up?*

*Just the moon, T-Boom, please. I'm sorry. I didn't
say—*

T-Boom had the moon in his hand, but he was

pulling that hand back away from me. And then I was grabbing for it but too fast, because T-Boom's hand was moving and we were both falling, his hand against my mouth hard and my elbow maybe against his.

T-Boom cursed, put his hand to his mouth, blood and a tooth with it.

When I sat up, my head hurt. My front tooth felt like it was freezing. I moved my tongue over it. Part of it was gone.

You chipped my tooth . . .

And mine is out of my head, so we're even. The end, he said, way too calm and quiet. Then his voice was loud again, loud and hard. *You're gonna destroy me.*

We sat staring at each other. I couldn't stop running my tongue over my tooth, couldn't stop wanting the moon to be inside me, making this all go away.

You're gone, Laurel, T-Boom said. His voice getting soft again, like there were tears somewhere behind it. *You weren't supposed to get like this. I trusted you. I trusted you!*

He threw the tiny package of moon at me.

Take it.

After another minute, he threw me his pipe and his lighter. The ground was cold underneath me, but the cold felt good, felt right. Then the moon was inside me, and I felt like I was on a carpet, drifting up over everything. Far away . . .

Let's do something, T-Boom. Let's go somewhere . . .

You can't even hear me anymore.

T-Boom got up and started walking away. I watched him go, slow motion and beautiful.

The moon moving so fast through me that I didn't see this beginning of the end of us. Didn't see the months coming at me—*You need to pay for it like everyone else does.* Didn't see his arm slipping forever from around my shoulder.

Let's go be crazy, T-Boom.

Didn't see his beautiful back already disappearing. His pretty, sad eyes no longer seeing me. *Gumbo* dark across a shoulder I wouldn't ever put my head against again.

Louisiana like a song . . .

Moon smoke so thick around me, like a blanket, like an arm . . . And me there on the ground

in the bright morning, staring out through it—
not knowing anything else anymore but this new
thing, this wanting nothing, needing nothing,
feeling nothing . . . but moon.

elsewhere

THE TELEVISION WAS ON, flashing news of the hurricane, when we walked into my Aunt G.'s house that evening. Cars had crawled a slow straight line up out of the Pass, and by the time we'd got to 49, the rain was already pounding down on us. Daddy was silent most of the way to Jackson, his jaw a hard, sad line, his fingers drumming the wheel. The one time Jesse Jr. cried, I pulled out one of the many bottles of formula Mama had made up for him. He watched me as he sucked on it—looking at me like I knew some answers he didn't. I chewed on pretzels and ate cheese sticks, trying hard not to think about Mama and M'lady back there in that rain.

As we pulled into Aunt G.'s driveway, she ran out, throwing her arms around my daddy, then me, then taking Jesse Jr. from my arms and rushing us all inside.

I'm sure y'all hungry. She was tall like my mama, had Mama's same blue-gray eyes.

I must have been staring at her, because she hugged me again, held me away from her, then pulled me to her one more time before letting go. Jesse Jr. made a sound in her other arm. She cradled him, kissed his forehead, her other hand still on my shoulder.

Water already coming hard on the Pass, she said. *They saying it's gonna be bad.*

My cousins came running down the stairs one right behind the other. They were all younger than me—three boys—Russ, Colvin and Daniel Jr.— and when they saw me standing there, they nearly knocked me over with their screaming and grabbing. Russell was the oldest—seven and already tall like his mama, but redheaded. Colvin was four, and Daniel Jr. was three, but they looked so much alike, most people thought they were twins. I remember when Daniel was born—Mama yelling to Daddy, *Gessie went and had herself another boy!* I let them jump all over me as I listened to Aunt G.

I've been praying on it, Aunt G. said, spooning coleslaw onto two plates, then piling them high with rice and sausage. *Mama and Marie are too stubborn. They should have both gotten out of there. Should be elsewhere.*

Daddy sat down at the table, holding the baby in one arm as he ate a piece of bread from the basket Aunt G. had put on the table. Jesse Jr. was awake, lifting his head up and trying to look around at everything. He smiled in my direction. Mama had said little babies couldn't see too far, but I swear he could smell me coming. He always knew just where I was.

Aunt G. put the two plates on the table, and I shook the boys off of me, washed my hands at the kitchen sink and sat down. Russell snatched up the chair on one side of me, and Colvin and Daniel fought over the other one. We bowed our heads, and my daddy said a prayer asking the Lord to keep everyone safe. When he was done praying, we opened our eyes. Jesse Jr. had fallen asleep again, but the boys sat there, watching me eat like they hadn't seen me in a million years.

Turn your big eyes away from me already, I said to them. *Y'all act like you never saw me before.*

The boys laughed but kept on staring, their eyes wide open like they were trying to drink every little bit of me in.

Strange to be somebody's favorite that way, for the first time. Long before Jesse Jr. grew up and loved me that hard.

Aunt G. brought a small bassinet over to the table, and Daddy closed his eyes and pressed his lips against the baby's head for a moment before settling Jesse Jr. into it.

The television was turned up in the living room, and we all listened while we ate. The newspeople were predicting heavy flooding, and the boys looked hard at me.

Lord have mercy, Aunt G. whispered. *Get them elsewhere, dear God. Get them on out of there.*

Mama and M'lady gonna be okay, Daddy?

They'll be all right, Daddy said real soft. *They*

going up to the Walmart if the water gets too high. They got a plan. He let out a heavy breath. *They'll be all right,* he said again. *They'll get somewhere else if they need to.*

But my daddy's hand trembled when he lifted his fork to his mouth. And Jesse Jr. woke up suddenly. And cried and cried and cried.

leaving galilee

THE FIRST TIME I hitched a ride to Donnersville, I was high on the moon. A woman pulled over to the side of the road and said I needed to get in before the rain came. Maybe I thanked her, I don't know. I pressed myself hard against the passenger side of her car and told her she could drop me off in the next town.

Which one? she asked.

I tried to look straight ahead but couldn't keep my head still. Felt like I wanted to look in every direction at once.

I got people in the next town, I said. *I ran out of money. Just need to borrow a few dollars from them.*

They in Donnersville? the woman asked. She said her name was Marcia and that she lived close to there.

Yeah. Donnersville.

But that's seven miles away, she said. *Next close town is Bradley.*

Donnersville, I said again. *They live in Donnersville.*

beneath
a meth moon

WIND BLOWING, and I'm high.

I'm high. I'm flying over everybody. I'm singing a song about a mountain. I am a mountain now, I'm high . . .

Fly 'cause you can be high when you fly. Fly 'cause the world will just pass you right by if you don't die.

I don't want to die being high. I don't want to die out here under the sky. But I'm high. Letting all the people pass me right by. Sing it with me—I'm high . . .

I'm high.

Turn it down just a little bit, like a whisper. *I'm high. I'm high. I'm high* . . .

donnersville

I CELEBRATED my fifteenth birthday sitting in the rain begging for money. I was living in Donnersville by then. Nights inside that room in back of the hardware store, days walking and begging for money. Always Mama's voice inside my head whispering, *Daneaus don't lie, and they don't steal,* so loud and hard that a part of me wanted to scream, *Then I'm not a Daneau anymore!* But scared always that the voice would go away, that her hand on my back, when I was shaking and sick with the need for moon, would lift off and disappear. Forever and ever. Amen.

On moonless days, I just went back to the empty

room, let the hurt become a part of someone else's story . . .

Once upon a time, there lived a girl named Laurelei, who was growing up with aching bones. Bones so painful, like an old woman. Blue bones, she called them, because, when the pain came, that was the color she saw. Blue-boned Laurelei . . .

My words filling up those peeling gray walls, filling up the spaces between other words in old magazines, filling up the insides of candy bar wrappers and paper peeled off of jars and napkins and paper bags and thrown-away envelopes—anything I could find to write on and write with. The notebooks M'lady had promised to always buy me no longer coming. M'lady no longer coming . . .

I'll buy you something pretty.

Pieces of other people's poems always rushing toward me.

I will arise and go now, and go to Innisfree.

Where was Innisfree? Did the poet ever get there?

Writing and pacing and writing and pacing till the words erased the pain. *The Pass comes back,*

Laurel. The water, the light, you and your daddy watching those fishing boats come in. Jackson. Aunt G.'s laughter coming from far off, telling you how much you favor your mama. The Pass comes back, Laurel. The Pass comes back. Till the voices quieted down and the water stopped rushing in.

Until sleep came, bringing tomorrow with it.

erase me

MOON TAKES MOST of your hunger away, to make more space for itself. Candy bars and soda, a peanut butter sandwich and some water, a bag of sour cherry balls—most days just a little bit of something was enough. By the time I'd been living for a while in Donnersville, I was thin and hollowed out. My hair hanging yellowed and clumping down over my back. Each time I saw myself in the storefront windows, I looked away real quick—thinking that wasn't me—that girl with the clothes hanging off her that way, her cheekbones jutting out of her face, her eyes sinking in . . .

Stay beautiful, my mama had said. And behind

her, M'lady kept saying, *I'll buy you something pretty. I'll buy you something pretty.*

So I stopped looking at my reflection. Without the store glass to look into, all that was left to look at was the walls I walked past. So many painted walls.

On the corner of Main and West Street, there was a painting of a dark-haired girl—her eyes like hard blue stones, her mouth soft, though—pale pink lips curling up. And inside the picture were the words

SERENITY LORETTA CHAPMAN

1990–2009

YOU'RE IN GOD'S HANDS, OUR LOVE.

MAMA & DADDY

And just below the Donnersville county line, there was a white building with a DANNY TACE, ATTORNEY AT LAW sign hanging. On the side of that building, you could see a small painting of a boy with glasses and short blond hair.

DANIEL TACE JR.

1979–2009

BLESSED BE. BLESSED BE.

Then, further in town, another sign, another girl—she was dark-haired too but gray-eyed and smiling.

LESLIE.

WE LOVE YOU. NOW AND ALWAYS.

APRIL 6, 1993—UNTIL THE SWEET HEREAFTER . . .

And always, at the bottom, far in the corner, were the initials *MS*.

Moses Sampson.

the second coming of moses

THEY PAY ME. *They tell me what to say. They give me the pictures of their kids. Sometimes they're still mad about it. Sometimes they can hardly talk from the sadness. You got any family somewhere?* he asked. He had been down the street, finishing up his painting of Ben. He was right—Ben was beautiful. Moses had painted wings on him, and there was something to the painting that made Ben look like he'd always been an angel. When Moses saw me, he stopped painting, put the cap on his spray can and came over.

He was wearing shades and pushed them up on top of his head with the back of his hand.

I looked off, didn't say anything. The wind picked up, and I pulled my jacket tighter around me. The jacket was old, dark blue with a small hole at the shoulder. There was a patch on the pocket that said LEADERSHIP ACADEMY. I'd gotten it from the free bin at the shelter I'd stayed at a few times. It was hard not to touch that patch and wonder who the jacket belonged to before me.

I know you said your people dead and gone, but you must be somebody's little girl, Moses said.

I'm fifteen. I'm not somebody's little girl.

Fifteen's not old, he said.

Not young either.

Moses said, *I know. I'm just wondering when your people are gonna come looking for me, asking me to paint your mural. Could do a good job with you. I'd probably start with snow because the first time you showed up around here, snow was coming down.*

I ignored him. Looked across the street at the mural he'd painted.

How come you not with your girl today?

Moses laughed. *My girl? What girl?*

That girl you were with yesterday. That black girl who said, "C'mon, Moses. We gotta go."

He shook his head. *That's not my girl! That's my crazy sister. Look how much love I put into Ben. Is that a sign of somebody who's into girls? C'mon, now.*

I looked away again. For some reason, it made me feel good that she was his sister and not his girl. And it made me feel good that he didn't like girls, wouldn't try to be getting something out of me.

You gonna give me two dollars, or you gonna waste my time?

You the one asking the questions about girls and whatnot. I was just minding my business, finishing up this angel. What if I said this is my part of the street now, you need to move on?

I'd keep sitting. I didn't say "because I don't have anyplace else to go." Didn't say "this is probably the end of the line for me, this piece of sidewalk in Donnersville."

You gonna give me two dollars? I asked again. The writing hardly came to me anymore—the words were crooked and crazy. I'd forgotten how to spell easy stuff, and when the voices came, the stories got all blurry before I could even write them down.

Maybe three dollars, Moses said. *You answer my question about who your people are. Three dollars will get me a hundred dollars in a few months, since you'll be dead at the rate you sucking down that meth. I don't even give you that long.*

You see me doing meth? You see me sucking on something? I'm just trying to eat! You never seen nobody trying to eat before?

Moses shook his spray can, then turned and started walking off, back toward his sign. I'd seen that walk before. Kaylee'd walked away from me like that. I'd seen that kinda *go* before. That *I'm done, I'm finished. I don't know you anymore.*

Marie and Charles Jesse Daneau, I said real soft. Maybe Moses didn't hear me, because he kept walking. So I said it louder. And then he stopped. Turned around.

They live here in Donnersville? Moses reached inside his back pocket. Took out his wallet, started to open it and waited.

Marie doesn't. I pointed up. *Preacher said she's watching over me.*

Moses got quiet. After a moment, he came back over, sat down beside me, put his spray can in his bag and folded his arms around his knees. His skin was dark brown like his jacket. Maybe he was seventeen. Maybe older. He had thick black eyebrows. Dark brown eyes.

I think a lot of the ones I'm painting had some kinda roughness in their lives. Small town like this—you figure you know. He pointed to Ben. *I knew him. Skateboard dude. He said when he was on his board, felt like he was flying.* Moses looked at his fingers. They were covered with paint. Mostly black, but red and green too. He stared at them like he was looking for something. *Knew a couple of the other kids, too.*

I picked up my hat and poured the little bit of change from it into my hand. Counted it real slow and put the money in my pocket. I studied my own fingers, like I was seeing the stains on them for the first time. My fingertips were yellow, like I'd been smoking for a million years. Seems that's what I was always doing now—chasing the moon—trying to catch the high, trying to hold on to it. Trying to step deep into it. And disappear.

You lose your mama to meth? I could probably do something simple for her. Cheap.

I almost laughed, then quick covered my mouth

with my hand. Mama never even took vitamins. The idea of Mama smoking the moon brought tears to my eyes—laughing/crying tears that I wiped away real fast.

The water came, I said. *Carried her away.* I got up, dumped the change from my hat into my bag and pulled the hat on over my hair. It was a dark green cotton cap. There were thick black stripes going round it. Some hat a skater kid probably lost. *I need to go.*

Moses looked up at me. *You called me back here. Now you're running off. Chasing your monkey.*

I didn't call you back!

Yes, you did, he said real soft. *You called out your people's names.*

Far off, I could hear sirens. Otherwise, there wasn't anybody on the street. No one walking past us. I looked down at my hands, how skinny and pale my wrists looked, my cold hands shaking, yellow fingertips uglier than anything. The moon was going out of me too fast, hurting me. I felt tired and jumpy all at once. *The water came and carried her away.* I heard the words moving around in my head, whispering themselves to me, then shouting. I heard the water rising up. Over me. Shook my head hard not to see again the flattened Walmart, water-stained and gone.

Moses reached in his pocket and handed me a tissue. I hadn't known I'd been crying until I took it from him, wiped my eyes, closed them tight again.

It get all your people? he asked.

I shook my head. It was getting dark. A few cars drove past us. A girl who looked to be about Moses's age walked by carrying a baby. Another kid was following close behind her. Younger than Jesse Jr. He looked at us, then ran and caught up with the girl.

Not my daddy. Not my brother either.

Then we need to find your brother and your daddy, don't we?

They . . . I know where they are.

Yeah—but do they *know where* you *are?*

I didn't answer. Just sat down again and pulled my legs up, wrapped my arms around them and stared out at the street. My face itched. I held tight to my own hands to keep from scratching. My teeth hurt like someone had tried to hammer them deeper into my gums. I tried to take my mind off of everything, tried to figure out how much more begging I'd have to do before I had enough money to head over to the Donnersville House, where the guy selling didn't give anybody a break the way T-Boom did. Mostly I was going over to the Donnersville House. Closer. Moon faster to come by there. No long walking to T-Boom. But when I didn't have enough money, I went back, begging T-Boom for a break.

Streetlamps were flickering on. Looked like lightning bugs the way they hesitated for a long time, flickering on and off like they were waiting for the right signal from somewhere. Ben's face flickered pale and dark again—over and over.

I gotta go, I said to Moses. The streetlights were all the way on now. Even with them, the street was dark, shadowy.

Stuff's hard to get off of. But you're young. It won't be deep for you. How long you been using—a few months?

Like you know. You just painting signs. You don't know.

I see you in snow, he said again. *Snow falling all around you. I see the flakes becoming your hair.*

He pulled his wallet out of his bag and opened it.

I thought he was going to take out some money, but instead he pulled out a picture of a woman. She was dark like him, pretty.

Wanna know where she is? I looked at him, and he pointed up. *County sent me and my sister here to Donnersville. Living with white folks we never seen in our lives. But they fed us, dressed us, took us to church and schooled us. My sister is everything they could pray for in somebody who "they gave a new life to." They're still trying to figure me out, though. So don't say "like you know." 'Cuz, truthfully, baby sis—you're the one who don't know.* He snapped his finger at me, then put the picture back in his wallet.

How? I whispered. My voice sounded like it was coming from somebody else. A faraway somebody.

How what?

How'd she . . . die?

Moses got quiet. Felt like a long time passed before he answered.

Her heart stopped when I was five. But she'd been doing meth for a while before that, so the way I figure it, her heart had stopped working, stopped loving, long before it stopped beating.

I painted her with a rainbow—but I put the rainbow way in the distance and her reaching toward it. I just wrote "Mama." No years. No God or Love stuff. Just "Mama." It's back in Fort Chester. Where we lived before we came here. First one I ever did.

He pulled three new dollar bills from his wallet and handed them to me. My hand was shaking as I took the money.

My sister said, "You can't save that girl, Moses. You don't have magic powers." And you know what? I bet she's right. I bet you gonna head right over to wherever it is you go and get high. I bet you gonna spend the rest of the spring sitting in front of this closed-up building growing more and more invisible to people.

Then what? I said.

Then you die, my lovely. He said it matter-of-fact, like it was the most obvious thing in the world. *Then somebody's gonna tell your daddy about the queer kid over in Donnersville who can paint a memory on a wall—just pay him for the painting, and the county will find him a wall. The county's happy to fill up empty walls with meth angels. Part of their anti-drug thing.*

They see me, I said. *I'm not invisible.*

They see a meth head. And some of them maybe see a little bit of a girl who used to be you in there. But most of them see a meth head and keep on walking because they got their own problems. That's what my sister said to do—keep on walking. And wait for your daddy to come looking for you with a picture of you.

Then how come some of them give me money if I'm so invisible?

Because they're hoping they'll give you enough to make you disappear. They hope they can walk by here one day and not see you. And when you're gone—even though they know in their hearts it's because you died on that crap, they can make believe you got clean and their little coins helped it happen. That's why.

He got up and brushed off the back of his jacket.

The strangest part of it is I'm already seeing you as a memory. Already seeing you fading on a wall . . . and I don't even know your name yet. Makes me sad for you.

You don't even know me. Just 'cuz you give me this money doesn't—

I do know you. You're disappeared just like a lot of us. Invisible. Just like a lot of us! Hated. Just like a lot of us! Don't tell me I don't know you. Your pain is SO not new.

He got up, put his bag on his shoulder. There were some paintbrushes sticking out of it. I could hear cans rattling inside.

What's your name, anyway?

He looked at me. He had a way of looking that made him seem old. I could almost see what he'd be like in fifty years—gray haired, wrinkled, with those same intense eyes.

I didn't say anything.

You still have one?

Laurel.

Moses nodded. *Pretty name. Laurel Donald—*

Daneau!

Laurel Daneau. Your people must have loved you lots to give you a name like that. You even know what Laurel is?

I'm not stupid.

Stays green forever, he said, like he hadn't heard me. *Even when there's winter all around it. Sits there like some kind of promise of spring.* He looked at me. *I bet there's still some spring in you, Ms. Daneau.*

He started walking away again. I watched him. He walked real slow, his head down, his whole body bending against the night and late spring Donnersville wind. I shivered thinking about what he'd said, thinking about summer and wondering if I'd live to see it.

daneau's girl

RAIN CAME HARD that first time I went into rehab, and by late afternoon, small rivers were moving along the sides of the building, puddling all around me. I sat up against the hardware store, shivering in my coat, my hat pulled down, my sign HOMELESS AND HUNGRY perched and sogging against my knees. The street was empty. The sky near black with clouds. I listened to the voices inside my head, the story of a girl skipping home through a big field—sunflowers all around her. I'd never seen a sunflower in real life. The story faded in and out of my brain. I shivered hard, trying to hold on to it—hold on to the sun coming down in that girl's field, the warmth all around her. Moses's eyes came to mind, the warm brown of them, and I tried to hold that thought too, him sitting next to me, us just talking. *I bet there's still some spring in you* . . . But soon, the warm brown and the soft words faded out of my brain and the rain was back, gray and cold.

A police officer stopped in front of me, dark shades hiding his eyes, a dollar bill hanging from his hand. Felt like I had to look up forever to finally see the top of his head, and when I did, I noticed how he'd tipped his hat forward. Clear plastic was covering the hat, and I thought that was strange— all the rain falling and the only thing protected from it was his hat, his long black coat left to soak up all that water.

Ladies' shelter no more than five blocks from where you're sitting, he said, holding the dollar out to me a minute longer. I didn't reach for it. I wasn't stupid enough to take money from a cop that way.

I got a home. I stared straight up at him, trying to see past those dark shades, that plastic-covered hat.

He nodded. *Yeah. And I got a million dollars. You*

need to get somewhere, because this rain's not stopping anytime soon. Calling for more coming—maybe even some flooding—and you're already shivering.

I pulled my arms tighter around me and closed my eyes hard, my breath coming fast. The flood coming again, and me with no place to go. The flood coming, and where was Daddy and Jesse Jr.? Where was everybody? The water was rising up, and this time it was gonna get all of us.

Help me, I whispered, pressing myself into the building behind me. *Help me . . .*

The cop hunched down closer to me and lifted his shades, water dripping from them, from his plastic hat, from everywhere. I couldn't move. Where could I run to if the water was already here?

Please . . .

His eyes got soft when he looked close at me.

Jesus! he said. *You're a kid!* He looked at me a moment longer. *Didn't you used to cheer for the Tigers?* he asked real slow. *Over in Galilee?*

I kept looking away from him.

My God! You're Charles Jesse Daneau's girl, aren't you?

I scratched at my face. It was hot suddenly. Itchy.

He pulled out his phone and started dialing.

You remember my son, Bernie? Point guard. You must know him. Jesus!

I got up slow, ready to run, but Bernie's daddy put his hand on my shoulder, hard. Holding me there. Each breath I took was filled with water. I was already drowning. Already sinking.

I remember your hair, he said, holding the phone to his ear with his other hand. *Nobody could miss your hair.* He looked at me hard for a long time. *Your daddy and brother been sick to death over you. Got the whole church praying you come off this stuff!* He turned away from me, speaking fast and quiet into his phone. I heard him say *Daneau's girl.* I wanted to try to run again, but hearing him say my daddy's name like that took every bit of energy out of me. I felt my stomach turning over. There was nothing in it, but something bitter was moving up to my throat. Bernie's dad let go of my shoulder for a moment to push his shades up, then quick grabbed me again. He had Bernie's same hard jaw. *My God*, he said. *How did this happen to you?*

the missing

BERNIE'S FATHER called a police car in from Galilee and put me in the backseat when the two cops showed up. The car was warm and smelled like coffee. But the rain was slamming against the windows, and I had to close my eyes tight to keep it away from me. One of the cops said, *You hungry?* and I shook my head no. I heard the other cop say, *Meth is food, clothing and shelter to these kids, you know that.*

I pressed my hands hard against the seat, trying to keep my whole body from twitching. My head hurt with all the things running through it. I couldn't remember the last time I'd eaten a meal.

The Heath bar I'd had at lunchtime was still turning around in my stomach, and I prayed that it wouldn't decide to make its way back up inside the car. And now, with the storm coming . . . what did M'lady and Mama eat before they died?

Bernie's dad went around to the front and said something to the driver. I opened my eyes to see both cops nodding at him. Bernie's dad waved to me as we pulled away, but I didn't wave back, just closed my eyes again, waiting for the water to come.

Your daddy meeting you at New Sunrise, Driver Cop said. *This your first time there?*

What's that? I said. *What's New Sunrise?*

Yup—her first time, I heard the other cop say.

Treatment. Help you kick this thing.

I don't have anything to kick.

Won't be her last time, Other Cop said, very matter-of-fact. Like he had all the answers to everything.

Over near Galilee, Driver Cop said. *They got a lot of these places right near each other. There's a lot of you, in case you haven't been noticing.*

We drove awhile with no one saying anything.

I'd seen other kids around the House and in Don-nersville, but none of us talked to each other much. Seemed everyone loved the moon in their own soli-tary way and didn't want to share.

I lay back against the seat again and closed my eyes. My jaw hurt, and I realized I'd been clenching my teeth. I hadn't seen my daddy in more than a month. Felt like a long time ago he'd stopped try-ing to find me, stopped dragging me home, stopped praying over my bedside, stopped believing . . . *What more's there to believe in?* he'd said the last time he caught me sneaking out to meet up with T-Boom. *Even when you're here, you're gone.* Then he closed the door. Maybe he watched through the window as I ran. I don't know. I missed him and Jesse Jr. like crazy when I let the missing take me. Most times I erased the thoughts coming before they could hit me too hard.

The day my daddy let me walk out of that house for the last time was the first time I heard him curse. The house filled with the smell of the moon I'd been smoking, and me so high I could hardly see him. Jesse Jr. in his pajamas, even though it was daytime. *I'm hungry, Daddy,* he kept saying over and over. *I'm so hungry.* And me so high I didn't need food, so I figured he didn't either. The food money gone . . .

Who had I become?

new sunrise

DADDY AND JESSE JR. were standing on the stairs when the cop car pulled up in front of a small white building with NEW SUNRISE painted across the door in thick black letters. I stared past him—just looked at the sign, trying not to see how old his face had gotten. How broken up he was. His beard was filled with gray and looked shaggy. When he first started growing it, he'd brush it every day, clip it— to keep it looking good, he'd said. He looked pale, and there were dark circles under his eyes. He was wearing a clear plastic poncho. Underneath it, he only had on a shirt and wrinkled pants. The pants were too long, dragging wet on the ground. I closed my eyes. The last time I'd seen him, he was cursing me, and now he was standing there, his clothes hanging big on his body, Jesse Jr. beside him, his coat soaking wet and too small. They watched me climb out of the cop car and then Jesse ran toward me. It was then the tears finally found a way to get out of me. Jesse's pale arms coming way past his sleeves, reaching up for me. *Lift me up, Laurel. Carry me! I want you to carry me!* I lifted him, and he threw his arms around me, hard and tight, tucking his nose into my neck like he used to do when he was small and scared. He'd grown taller, his legs hanging down near my knees. His hair had gotten long and dark, sticking to his neck in dirty clumps.

I felt my daddy's hand on my shoulder and pressed my face into his coat, and the three of us stood there for a long time, the cops just watching.

I lied, Daddy, I whispered. *I do need the moon. Please, please help get it out of me . . .*

My daddy's tears against my face warm as rain.

lord, do remember me

NEW SUNRISE IS IN SUMMITVILLE off of Route 38, just down the highway from a school for the blind and across the street from a Walmart. The first day there, I stared out the small window in my room, imagining the water washing over Walmart and floating it down the highway. Over and over again, the water came in and washed the big white building with its huge blue letters away. The *W* and *A* and *L* floating past me.

They made me say good-bye to Daddy at the door. Behind him, Jesse Jr. stared at me, his small face pressed against my daddy's leg, his eyes wide and afraid.

You gonna come home again, Laurel? Jesse Jr. asked me. *You gonna live with us again?* I promised him I would. Then Jesse Jr. and Daddy were driving away, back home, to wait for me to come home from New Sunrise, moon-free and Laurel again.

A woman named Esther showed me to my room up a long flight of stairs and at the end of a long hall of rooms.

There aren't any locks, Esther said. *We trust in you and the Lord to keep you here, but we can't lock you in. Your journey is your own. But everyone at New Sunrise loves you already, Laurel. We're here to guide you home.*

I'll give you some time to get settled, Esther said as she went through my pockets, made me take off my shoes and pulled the soles back to look beneath them. The cops had taken my pipe and moon away. There wasn't anything left for her to find. In my knapsack I just had my filled-up writing books and three pens, a bunch of scrap paper with lots of words written all over each piece, and a slice of bread and cheese I'd gotten that morning at the Salvation Army breakfast cart.

Would you like to pray now? Thank the Lord for your journey? She smiled at me. She was tall and skinny. Maybe she was twenty-five, but her face was hard and old-looking, and I knew from looking at her that she'd once known the moon.

I thanked Him already, I lied.

Then I'll see you in an hour at meeting, Esther said. *Stay blessed.*

I lay down on the bed and tried to pray—*We know not the day nor the hour. Lord, do remember me. Our Father who art in Heaven, give us . . .* but the words tumbling out of me didn't make sense, and when the tears started coming, I couldn't stop them. I was shivering and burning up all at once. My skin was prickling all over like some invisible thing was taking bites out of me. I scratched hard at any part I could reach.

I don't know how long I stayed that way, scratching and crying, but when I got up off the bed, my throat was burning and the sky was black. The storm was right there—waiting to pour down over me. Maybe I was ready—ready to let it. Felt like it'd been years of me running from the storm and now it'd found me, now it'd come to take me. I was tired. I couldn't run anymore.

I walked slow to meeting, sat down in a circle surrounded by other people who knew the moon. We prayed. We held hands. So many people cried when they told their stories. A girl just a little bit older than me who had known the moon since she was nine. We looked at each other. Looked away from each other. Maybe she could have been a friend to me, but I didn't need any friends anymore. I just wanted sleep—sleep until the storm washed me away.

Days passed, and the Walmart sign was always just outside my window. When it rained, everything looked like it was melting. Maybe I was melting. Maybe that was how I'd disappear. When the thoughts came hard—Jesse Jr. crying in my arms, the too-long, wet cuffs on my daddy's pants, Mama and M'lady—I wrote. Wrote until my hand hurt, wrote until the itching didn't bother me, until the memories didn't hurt coming on . . . wrote about the happy endings and people laughing, about sun on water and people's hair—I wrote about Kaylee and the squad, about gumbo and shrimp boils, about M'lady taking out my hem and telling me about my future . . .

Laurel . . . ?

I'm here. I'm still here.

The moon staying inside me, pulling . . . pulling on me hard. Slowly, the sky cleared. Slowly, the storm passed over me.

Laurel . . . Your daddy and brother are here . . .

The day before I left New Sunrise, Daddy and Jesse Jr. came to see me. They made us sit in a meeting room with a counselor. We were supposed to sit in chairs in a small circle and talk about family problems that made me chase the moon. But Jesse Jr. only wanted to sit in my lap, his arms tight around my neck. *You have to sit in your own seat,* the counselor kept saying. She wasn't the woman from my first day. She was older, a psychologist or something. Dr. Somebody.

You're not the boss of me, Jesse Jr. said. *Laurel is the boss of me.*

I held tight to Jesse Jr., not wanting to let him go. My daddy sat across from us, watching me. He'd shaved off his beard, but he still looked older, tired.

When the counselor finally gave up on Jesse Jr. leaving my lap, she asked my daddy how he was doing.

I just want Laurel to live, he whispered. *I just want her to make it.* He looked at me. *I'd give my whole life for that, baby girl. My whole life.*

I didn't know how to say to him that I didn't want his life. I didn't want to lose anybody else—couldn't live if another somebody died on me. I held tight to Jesse Jr. Put my face deep in his warm neck, sniffed the smells of him—sweat and something a little bit sour and sweet at the same time.

I'm not mad at you, Laurel, my daddy said. *Been too worried sick about you to be anything but worried sick. But when I'm not worrying and fretting about you, I'm remembering my baby girl, the wind blowing in your hair, how you used to make me lift you up so you could grab some sky and put it in your pocket . . .*

His voice dropped off, and even though I couldn't look at him, I knew he was crying, crying like he'd cried when we came up on where our house used to be in the Pass, crying like he did when we found out Mama and M'lady didn't make it, crying hard like he'd cried at the funerals. I pressed my face hard into Jesse Jr.'s neck, thinking about how easy the moon made all that sadness lift up and fly away.

You gonna die, Laurel? Jesse Jr. had asked before him and my daddy left me at New Sunrise that day. *'Cuz then who would be my sister anymore?*

After they left, I went back into my room, lay on my bed and let the darkness take over. I used to ask M'lady what happened when you died, where'd your thinking go. *I don't really know where your thinking goes,* she'd answer. *Just your soul.* The moon took my thinking away, lifted it right up out of me and filled that space where it was with good things— light and sweetness. Happiness. When I was high, I was happy.

My hands were shaking as I put my notebooks and my pens and the pieces of paper into my bag. There was quiet all around me. Maybe it was midnight. The darkness was calling hard to me. Cool air all around me. And somewhere, I could hear a train whistle blowing low. Over and over again. Like it was telling me which way to run. So I did run, hard as I could, away from that place.

By the time I stopped running to catch my

breath, I was sweating. A few stars were out. Some clouds moved, revealing the moon. I ran half the night—toward it.

And T-Boom was there, like he knew I was coming.

laughter

I KNEW SCHOOL WAS OUT by all the kids walking past me. Some days, I saw whole groups of teenagers walking together. I'd gotten used to them walking by and laughing at me or crossing the street to ignore me. Sometimes I could see bits of the girls' bathing suits peeking out as they walked past me, and I knew they were heading to the water park. When we first moved to Galilee, we drove by a big sign for it, and I said to Jesse Jr., *I'm gonna take you there one day.* Now here it was summer, and I didn't even know where he was, how he was doing . . . if anybody else had come along and taken him there. Taken him anywhere . . .

You're still you in there, Laurel, Moses said each time he saw me, each time we sat for a moment and talked. *You always talk about all that light in Pass Christian. But you're trying to forget that y'all brought a couple of sparks with you. None of them shining in that dark nasty room you're calling home now, my girl. You need to stop moving toward the darkness.*

There was a clothing store across the street from where I sat, and one day, I watched a mama and her little girl go into it. A little while later, they came back out, the little girl letting her bag hit against her leg again and again as she skipped ahead, her mama smiling down at her. I tried to remember if that was ever me and Mama, but all that came to me was us together at the Dollar Store where Mama worked, me walking slow up and down the aisles, looking at the dollar toys and candies and nail polishes. Seemed that place was a whole other world to me, and on paydays, when M'lady took me there, Mama would smile real big when she saw us come through that door. *Get whatever you want, Laurel,* she'd say. *Everything's a dollar, but that's before the employee discount.* And then my mama would laugh as I grabbed armloads of balloons and plastic horses, stickers and M&M's. *Bless her heart, M'lady, Mama would say. Laurel's the first Daneau to go on a true-blue shopping spree.*

And then, more laughter. Laughter that seemed to go on and on. Filling up the Dollar Store, floating right out of that store and into the big wide world.

moses
and rosalie

MOSES WAS CARRYING a green nylon bag when he walked up to me.

There was a loaf of bread sticking out of his bag, two paintbrushes poking out beside it. When he asked me if I wanted the end of it, I laughed, remembering how I used to offer the end to Jesse Jr. He'd always say yes, and I'd break it off for him, let him eat it as we walked home.

You not painting anybody today?

Moses shook his head.

Yesterday I finished Rosalie's. Rosalie Wright. I knew her. I met her when I first came to Donnersville. She was thirteen. She said she loved me. Moses took a deep breath and looked out over the empty street. He got real quiet, and it was like nobody was there— not me, not anybody else either. Just him—deep in someplace nobody could go to with him. *I told her I didn't like her. Not that way.*

Did you love her any kind of way? I asked real quiet.

Moses nodded. *Yeah.* After another minute passed, he said, *I didn't know how to say it, though. I was just figuring everything out. And the figuring was coming slowly.*

There were queer kids at school. I'd never met any until I moved to Jackson. M'lady had said being that way was against everything natural, and I hadn't thought anything about it until I got here. Daddy's older brother was . . . strange. That's what M'lady called him, the few times he came to visit from California. *He's strange, Laurel. Different.* And it wasn't till I got to Jackson and got older there and listened to Aunt G. and Daddy talking that I realized Uncle Jimmy's strangeness was the same strangeness Moses had. Wasn't till I was sitting in front of Aunt G.'s television, listening to their low talking coming from the kitchen, that

I remembered how Mama didn't pay any mind to what M'lady said about Uncle Jimmy. *And you don't need to pay any mind to it either, Laurel,* she said to me. *Don't pay any mind to mean talk anybody says about anybody.* Sitting in front of that television, Mama already buried, I thought about how Uncle Jimmy loved Mama like a sister. At her funeral he cried like a baby.

Now here was Moses, strange like Uncle Jimmy, strange like the boys at school in Jackson who had their own club, threw their own parties and wore T-shirts that said NOTHING TO HIDE and KISS A FAIRY, who got beat up sometimes and sometimes beat people up, but everyone just kept on moving, everyone just . . . kept being. Here was Moses, strange and good—dropping money in my hat, bringing me bread, sitting to talk awhile. Here was Moses . . . strange . . . and here now.

I decided I needed a day off, Moses was saying. *Rosalie's around the corner, if you want to see her.*

I did. I got up from the bench and walked to the end of the street, then turned and walked a little ways more. On the side of a dark gray building, there was Rosalie's face. She was dark like Kaylee, with beautiful dark eyes. Moses had painted her turned to the side a little, and a tiny dimple showed at the top of her cheek. She was smiling. Not smiling, laughing, and it felt like I could hear her laughing right there on the road—coming at me all high and pretty.

Something caught in my chest—something that made it hard to take a breath, to swallow. I stared at Rosalie until I couldn't see her anymore—until her face was melting down off that wall, into the street, disappearing. And then I noticed Rosalie had my same birthday. My same year . . .

I started running then, hard—away from Rosalie, away from Moses. Hard and fast as I could, with the hot wind on my face, drying the tears quick-fast as they came. I ran until the buildings disappeared, until the street turned to dirt and the dust kicked up into my throat. But I kept running. Fast as I could . . . away from that wall, my birthday up there for everybody to see me already dead. Running away from being already dead. Knowing I was dead dying gone. Running to keep on living. So, so scared to die . . .

home's a place
i used to know

AUNT G. HELD JESSE JR. in her arms as me and Daddy got in the car for the long drive back to the Pass. It was warm out, blue and clear after the hurricane. Rain was still coming down in the Pass, but I couldn't imagine it, couldn't imagine all the water the newscasters were talking about.

All week long, we'd glued ourselves to Aunt G.'s television, waiting for news about the storm. Over and over, we saw the water washing over Mississippi, watched the people cry about what they'd lost, heard the crash of the levees breaking in Louisiana, followed the eye of the storm.

And all week long we called home. *Don't worry,*

Mama said the first night after we left, even as the phone line broke up, sending her voice in a lot of directions at once. *We're. Fine. Here. Dry as bones. And. Having. Ham and rice for dinner.* But the next day, no one answered. Every hour, the phone going straight to voice mail. And every other number of all our friends too. Daddy dialing and redialing, slamming down the phone, then dialing again. Pacing Aunt G.'s kitchen, and Aunt G. with Jesse Jr. at the table. *It's gonna be all right, Charles. They got themselves somewhere. It's gonna be all right.* But me and Daddy dialed the numbers again and again, leaving messages till we couldn't anymore. Till the only voice we heard was the recorded one. *The voice mail is full. The voice mail is full. The voice mail is full.*

And the roads washed out and no way home. *Whose bad dream am I living?* Daddy whispered until the mayor said, *Come home and find your people and get your stuff. Then leave again.* So we were on our way. Home.

Ride up front with me, baby girl, my daddy said. So I climbed into the front seat of the car and watched the world coming at me. Green and thick with life.

Until the hours passed and we were close to the Pass. And nothing was familiar at all.

We crawled along slow, cops ahead stopping each car and bending down into it. Maybe an hour passed this way—Daddy with his hand covering part of his face, as though he knew what was coming.

No outsiders, the cop said.

We live here, my daddy said, looking straight ahead, his eyes half closed like he wanted to see and didn't at the same time. For as far as we could see, houses were flattened, roofs were blown off. Cars and trees turned over on their sides.

You got proof of address?

Daddy reached into his wallet and took out his driver's license. *We're coming back for my wife and mother-in-law,* he said, his voice shaking.

The cop gave him a long, sad look. *The houses along the water gone, sir,* he said. There was a hurt sound in his voice—loving, though, like the voice Daddy would use when I was little to convince me there wasn't a monster under my bed.

They went up higher, Daddy said. *To the Walmart— up off 49. We're gonna see if they're still there. Can't get no answer at home.*

The cop took a deep breath, then pulled a pad from his back pocket and wrote something down. He ripped out the page and handed it to my daddy.

You might want to go here first, he said real soft. *It's on your way. You can cover all your bases this way—instead of driving around and looking for people to ask.*

Daddy took the paper from him and looked at it, then looked back at the cop without talking for a long time. When he finally spoke, his voice was tinier than I'd ever heard it, like a small child's. *Why . . . why . . . don't understand why you'd send me to the morgue . . . Officer?*

The police officer took off his cap and squinted out over the long line of cars waiting to get back down to the water. He put his hand on the back of his neck, closing his eyes. When he opened them again, he looked old and very, very tired. *I'm not saying they're there, sir,* he said, his voice coming slow. *I'm saying it's on the way, and it seems to be where most people are looking first. This is the direction we're sending people.* A moment passed and then he said, *That's where they took the Walmart bodies, sir. I'm sorry.*

dream

IN THE DREAM, my teeth fall out, one by one until there's no more teeth in my head. Then I wake up screaming, but no one hears me. Again and again, inside the dream, I wake up screaming. Then I'm falling from somewhere high up. I wake up still falling.

That morning, though, I woke up from my falling thinking about Moses's Rosalie. Thinking about how you can be thirteen years old and in love with a boy, then be fifteen and dead and gone. And still laughing. Up on that wall, Rosalie was still laughing. I was awake but still falling . . .

I climbed up from the floor slowly. My body hurt.

Mostly my teeth had that hammered pain in them. The tiny room was hot and dark. I'd gotten used to sleeping on somebody's left-behind air mattress with no air in it, but the darkness always surprised me—how dark Donnersville could get at night. Pass Christian was more and more becoming just a memory to me, and the memory was mostly filled with light—sun off the water, sun beating down and coloring everything bright white.

It was raining out—hot, though. Maybe I'd been asleep off and on for two days. Maybe three. My stomach felt hollow. My throat burned. My heart just kept pounding and pounding.

The room let out into a broken-down yard. I stepped outside and let the rain pour down over me. Opened my mouth to quench the burning. There were some tires against a high fence and a patch of garden that was weeds mostly with some ivy creeping out of it and up the fence wall. I stood in the rain staring at that ivy, watching it climb over that wall and disappear. Some part of me wanted to follow it, keep on moving the way it kept on moving . . .

Don't know how long I stood there with my

clothes all wet and sticking to me, rain falling into my eyes, dripping from my hair, running down my back . . .

Don't remember when the rain stopped. When the sun came out. Don't remember writing the stuff about ivy down on some paper, drinking the rain, until I read about it in my notebook later on . . .

I thought you were dead, this time, Moses said.

I remember turning and seeing him standing there. Being surprised because he never came back here before.

I got bread and chocolate and oranges, he said. He had on a white T-shirt and long camouflage shorts with pockets on the side. I remember the pockets— how he pulled two oranges out of them and handed me one.

His hand holding that orange out to me.

And the way the mist sprayed into my face, surrounding me with the smell of orange and rain.

And us sitting down on that stack of tires, sharing the buttered rolls Moses pulled out of those pockets. Those pockets real big in my memory, never empty.

It scared me, thinking you were back in that room,

dead, Moses said. *Kept seeing myself finding you dead. Being the one to have to go to the police.*

Moses opened his roll and put a piece of chocolate between the bread. I watched him without saying anything. He took a bite and looked over the yard.

What kind of sandwich is that?

A chocolate sandwich, he said—like he was telling me it was a ham sandwich, something real familiar that I was a fool not having heard about. He pulled another piece of chocolate out of his pocket, unwrapped it and held it out for me to break off a piece. I put it in my roll and took a bite. It was nice the way the chocolate melted around the bread inside my mouth. I must have smiled, because Moses nodded.

We must have sat there for a long time, because my memory of the day goes from rain to sun. From day to near dark. My memory of it that's biggest, though, is how me and Moses sat and talked and talked and talked. And it wasn't till near night that I realized I had gone the whole day without the moon. Gone the whole day with bread and chocolate and oranges, and Moses, like this was how it'd always been. And always would be.

donnersville moon

MOSES WASN'T THERE in the morning, when I grabbed a stranger's sleeve and begged him for money. Wasn't there when the man looked in my face, and in pity dropped a twenty-dollar bill in my hand—then pushed me hard away from him.

Moses wasn't there when I ran drug sick to the small cabin in Donnersville, where the meth heads went, where the people who weren't me smoked the moon right outside, not caring. He wasn't there when I handed the strange kid hanging from the window the money, stood there hugging myself, my face and hands feeling like a million bugs were crawling all over me. He wasn't there as I stood there scratching till the blood ran down.

Wasn't there to see me crowded next to the meth heads, smoking the moon up until I couldn't breathe, until I couldn't see. Until the world disappeared in a white-hot light of pain and noise and my own voice screaming out, *I can't breathe! I can't breathe. Somebody help me. I can't breathe anymore!*

And then . . . nothing at all.

Where are you, Moses?

I'm looking for you.

Where is your bread? Where is your chocolate?

I'm looking for you, Laurel. I'm looking for you.

another
second chance

AND WHEN I WOKE UP in the hospital room, Daddy and Kaylee and Jesse Jr. were there—standing at my bedside, their eyes red and swollen, their smiles trembling. My head hurt, and my chest felt thick and heavy.

You messed up your heart, Laurel, Jesse Jr. said, coming to the edge of my bed. *But it's still working.*

And when I tried to move, I couldn't. And when I tried to hug him, I couldn't lift my arm.

You have to rest, my daddy said. He looked old standing there, more gray than I remembered, broken and unsure. *You got another long road ahead of you, baby girl.*

And for a moment, we just looked at each other, his eyes pleading, *Please make it this time.*

Does your heart still work to love me? Jesse Jr. asked, his tiny face so close I could smell the applesauce that he'd eaten.

It still works, I whispered, the words hurting as they came out of me, my throat burning, a new unfamiliar burn.

They had to incubate you, Jesse Jr. said.

Intubate, Kaylee said. *You've had a tube down your throat for a week. Did you feel it at all?*

Kaylee picked up my hand. There was a tube running up from my wrist along the inside of my arm. I couldn't tell where it stopped. I tried to squeeze Kaylee's hand.

You okay?

She nodded. *I'm not letting you leave me out in the country by myself again. You know that, right?*

I squeezed her hand again.

How about you? You gonna live to tell the story?

I smiled but couldn't answer her.

My daddy collapsed into the chair beside my bed and took a long, hard breath.

She's okay now, Daddy, Jesse Jr. said, patting my daddy's shoulder while Kaylee held tight to my hand. There was the sound of Daddy's tears and the sound of something close by beeping and the sound of nurses calling over the intercom, asking doctors where they were. The sound of life going on—and me there, in it.

Me there in it.

I'm okay, Daddy. I'm gonna be okay now.

She's gonna be okay, now, Daddy, Jesse Jr. echoed.

My father took deep breaths and nodded. He looked at me, his eyes so full of so many things I had to look away.

Is Moses here?

Who's Moses?

I closed my eyes. How would they know him? How would anybody know anything about that world I walked in? So far away from this one?

Is he the guy who found you? Kaylee asked. *They said somebody called the ambulance, said you were from Galilee.*

I was looking for you.

Are we in Galilee?

Kaylee shook her head. *Donnersville Hospital.* She bent down to kiss me on the forehead, her hair falling across my face. I tried to reach up to hold her. But couldn't. So I pressed my face against hers. *Give me your sun, Kaylee,* I wanted to say. *Take this pain away from me.* But only tears came.

elegy for mama and m'lady

THE MORNING WE LEFT Pass Christian, my mama came into my room and whispered, *You behave yourself at your cousins' house, Laur. Ask to help with dishes and make your bed without Aunt G. having to ask you, you hear me?*

I woke up slowly. It was still near dark outside. My mama had her hand on my face, looking down at me. Jesse Jr. had just turned three months old and was asleep in his crib across from me. He stirred, making tiny baby noises.

C'mon, Laur, time to get up now. I have to get the baby up and dressed. Get y'all on the road.

It wasn't until she was buckling Jesse Jr. into his

infant seat that it hit me she wasn't coming. I had heard them talking late into the night. I'd heard my daddy fussing with her. I'd heard M'lady saying, *I don't need anyone staying here with me.* And then I'd gone to sleep.

Soon as the rain is done, Daddy's gonna bring y'all back here, my mama said. She kissed the top of my forehead.

But, Mama—

Hush, Laur. Don't you wake that baby and start him to crying.

Jesse Jr. was just a baby, so I didn't know if Mama's tears were about him leaving her for the first time or seeing the tears in my own eyes. But she turned away from us, wiped her eyes real fast, then turned back again.

I don't want to hear that your aunt had to ask you to make your bed.

I nodded but couldn't speak. Couldn't look at her. M'lady sat swinging on the front porch.

Just gonna be a day or two, she said. *Don't know why you all falling apart so.*

That was the last time we saw them breathing.

daddy

I WANT TO SAY I remember leaving the hospital, remember the drive back to Galilee, my father in the front, humming along to the radio and me beside him. Jesse Jr. in the back talking nonstop, like he wanted to fill me in on everything I missed. I want to say I remember the way the sky turned clear blue as we drove and when I looked up into it, I thought, *This is what's beautiful about living—the way the world seems to go on and on.* I want to write that I left that hospital not wanting the moon, entered that rehab already done with it. But what I remember most is how it hurt to not feel my moon pipe against my lips, how the scratching scars on my face reminded me for a long time how the moon had made me itch and cry out. How, late some nights, I wanted to run from rehab back to the House, any House, and erase, erase, erase.

How I dreamed M'lady saying, *The moon will stand beside you with the Lord . . .*

But what comes clear to me each day is the morning my father came into Second Chances and handed me my knapsack, smiling. It was the first smile I'd seen on his face in a long time.

Your friend Moses brought this by, he said. *Bet you didn't know we're the only Daneaus in Galilee.*

Moses came to our house?

He said he wanted to make sure you got your stories back. He . . . saved . . . he saved . . . he saved you. My daddy's voice caught, but he shook his head, took a breath. *I know I keep saying it. Feel like I have to so I know it's true. He's going to come by here. See how you doing. I hope that's okay.*

Yeah, Daddy. I want him here. I want Moses to come see me. Tell him please come . . .

We got quiet for a minute. My daddy's hands on my face, looking hard in my eyes.

He never did the moon, I said. *His mama did, but not him. I don't want you thinking—*

I know, sweet pea. I didn't at first. When he rang our bell and had that bag, I was ready to kill him, ready to go to jail with all the mad inside of me. But he stood there, said real clear, "Mr. Daneau, my name is Moses. You don't know me, but you can find my name in the Donnersville hospital records." And that was all he needed to say before I threw my arms around that boy. Hugged him hard.

I nodded, not able to speak. My daddy kissed my forehead, like he used to do when I was little.

My hands were shaking as I unzipped the bag. It was filthy and smelled like the room I'd stayed in—musty and damp and meth-smoke sweet. I felt my stomach creeping up as I opened it, watching the months of notebooks and envelopes and paper bags and pieces of paper fall out.

I pulled a wrinkled envelope from the pile. The edges of it were brown, like maybe I'd held my lighter to it. *This is me,* I'd written. *In this room. High. Beneath a meth moon. My name is Laurel Daneau, and once upon a time . . . once upon a time . . . before the rain came and washed us all away . . .*

Laurel, my daddy said, *you held on to it, baby girl. You wrote it down. Don't cry like that, sweetie. It's the past. It's behind you now.*

My daddy sat down and I climbed into his lap like I was five instead of fifteen. Put my head against his chest and cried and cried. And my daddy held me. Held me like he was never gonna let me fall.

elegy

IT'S NOVEMBER NOW. Summer feeling like it's long behind me. Jesse Jr. holds tight to my hand as we walk the half mile to his day care center. Even when he skips ahead of me, he refuses to let go.

This is an elegy for Jesse Jr., who lived so many months without me. An elegy for the boy who lost his grandma and his mother and almost lost his sister, too.

In the pocket of my jeans is the medal I got from Second Chances—a small gold coin marking ninety days without the moon.

This is an elegy to the moon no longer running through my veins.

My pom-poms bounce against my legs, my

cheerleading uniform in my bag, the mighty Tigers will be waiting this afternoon, for me and Kaylee and the rest of the squad to cheer them on. Kaylee, coming over every evening, counting the days with me. Moonless days. Days till Texas or Colorado or wherever we go from here.

Some mornings I see T-Boom wandering the streets of Galilee, his eyes wild. *Hey, beautiful girl,* he says to me. *How about a dollar for the guy who loved you once. You know the House is blown up and gone now. They got me paying for it now. Crazy, huh?*

And sometimes I hand it to him.

I could help you move through it, T-Boom. You don't need the moon.

I know, he says. *I'm getting off this train. Gonna play ball again. Soon, baby, soon.* Then he's walking fast away from me.

This is an elegy for T-Boom and prayer for the ones who didn't make it.

In the distance, I hear a train whistle blowing and smile, thinking of Moses. In January he will leave Donnersville, heading to college in another town. *Psychology,* he said when I asked him what he plans to study. *Because you were my first successful patient. My golden girl.* But before he leaves, we'll spend many hours sitting by the train tracks, talking about our futures, talking about our past, a loaf of bread, a bar of chocolate and so much more between us.

At the corner of First and Holland, Jesse Jr. stops, pulls me down and kisses my cheek before we head inside. *You'll be here to get me later, right?* he asks, his brown eyes bright. *You'll be waiting for me?*

And I hold tight to him, because I know I'll be waiting for him, today and the next day and the one after that. Waiting and watching out for him until we're grown and gone from here.

Grown and gone from here.

I watch him skip into his day care center as his teacher waves to me from the top of the stairs. *He's a joy,* she says. And I smile, proud as Mama and M'lady would have been about what a joy Jesse Jr. is.

Later, after school, I'll shop for the ingredients for M'lady's gumbo—okra, sausage, chicken . . . the spices coming quick to my brain like I'd never forgotten them. By late afternoon the house will smell like Pass Christian . . .

As I turn and start walking, I hear M'lady's laughter coming toward me, and I can see her blue braid dancing over her back as she tosses her head toward heaven, saying softly, *Lord, girl, you surprise me every day.*

The wind picks up as I walk. The sound of it moving through the trees reminds me of the water, and I know that sound will always be inside of me, gentle as time.

Laurel! I turn to see Jesse Jr. standing there. *I need another kiss good-bye, please.* Then, while his teacher looks on, he runs back into my arms, hugs me hard as anything and kisses my cheek. Then I watch him walk back inside with his teacher, excited as any four-year-old can be about something new. I wave long after he's turned away from me, wave until my eyes blur and burn.

It's a long walk away from meth, my counselor said to me. *It's a slow walk. It's a hard walk.*

But I put one foot in front of the other. And I keep on moving.

If You Come Softly
ALA BEST BOOK FOR YOUNG ADULTS

★ "Once again, Woodson handles delicate, even explosive subject matter with exceptional clarity, surety and depth. . . . She seems to slip effortlessly into the skins of both her main characters. . . . The intensity of their emotions will make hearts flutter, then ache. . . . Even as Woodson's lyrical prose draws the audience into the tenderness of young love, her perceptive comments about race and racism will strike a chord with black readers and open the eyes of white readers."

—*Publishers Weekly*, starred review

"Woodson confronts prejudice head-on."   —*Booklist*

"Lyrical narrative. . . . This fine author once again shows her gift for penning a novel that will ring true with young adults as it makes subtle comments on social situations."   —*School Library Journal*

Behind You

YALSA QUICK PICK
YALSA TOP TEN BEST BOOKS FOR YOUNG ADULTS

★ "Poignant. . . . With tenderness and compassion, the author exposes the characters' vulnerabilities and offers the hope that they will emerge and grow from this tragic loss. . . . Readers who savor tough reality stories as much as happy endings will appreciate this thought-provoking, satisfying novel that offers hope but no easy answers."

—*School Library Journal*, starred review

"Moving. . . . Woodson writes with impressive poetry about race, love, death, and what grief feels like— the things that 'snap the heart'—and her characters' open strength and wary optimism will resonate with many teens." —*Booklist*

"Woodson plays the language of feeling with an often stunning virtuosity; her crystalline vision makes each voice herein resonate with its own particular emotional tone. . . . There are moments of real beauty in this melancholy yet ultimately life-affirming examination of grief."

—*The Bulletin of the Center for Children's Books*

Miracle's Boys
CORETTA SCOTT KING AWARD
LOS ANGELES TIMES BOOK PRIZE
ALA BEST BOOK FOR YOUNG ADULTS

★ "Readers will be caught up in this searing and gritty story. . . . Woodson composes a plot without easy answers."   —*Kirkus Reviews*, starred review

★ "Once again, Woodson reveals a keen understanding of the adolescent psyche. . . . An intelligently wrought, thought-provoking story."
—*Publishers Weekly*

★ "Compelling. . . . As usual, Woodson's characterizations and dialogue are right on. The dynamics among the brothers are beautifully rendered. . . . Powerful and engaging."   —*School Library Journal*

"Fast-paced narrative is physically immediate, and the dialogue is alive with anger and heartbreak."
—*Booklist*